A TALE OF TWO CITIES

VOLUME TWO OF TWO

A Tale of Two Cities
Dickens, Charles, 1812 – 1870
First Published by Chapman and Hall in 1859

Text edits © 2025 Grand Type Classics
Design © 2025 Grand Type Classics

Text set in 18 point Helvetica.
Chapter headings set in Helvetica Neue.

All rights reserved. All materials in this book are protected by copyright. No part of this publication may be reproduced, distributed, or transmitted in any form or by any means, including photocopying, recording, or other electronic or mechanical methods, without the prior written permission of the publisher.

ISBN: 978-1-83412-292-2 Volume One
ISBN: 978-1-83412-293-9 Volume Two

A TALE OF TWO CITIES

A STORY OF THE FRENCH REVOLUTION

VOLUME TWO OF TWO

CHARLES DICKENS

GRAND TYPE CLASSICS

CONTENTS

VOLUME ONE

VOLUME TWO

BOOK THE THIRD

The Track of a Storm

CHAPTER ONE

In Secret

THE TRAVELLER fared slowly on his way, who fared towards Paris from England in the autumn of the year one thousand seven hundred and ninety-two. More than enough of bad roads, bad equipages, and bad horses, he would have encountered to delay him, though the fallen and unfortunate King of France had been upon his throne in all his glory; but, the changed times were fraught with other obstacles than these. Every town-gate and village taxing-house had its band of citizen-patriots, with their national muskets in a most explosive state of readiness, who stopped all comers and goers, cross-questioned them, inspected their papers, looked for their names in lists of their own, turned them back, or sent them on, or stopped them and laid them in hold, as their capricious judgment or fancy deemed best for the dawning Republic One and Indivisible, of Liberty, Equality, Fraternity, or Death.

A very few French leagues of his journey were accomplished, when Charles Darnay began to perceive that for him along these country roads there was no hope of return until he should have been declared a good citizen at Paris. Whatever might befall now, he must on to his journey's end. Not a mean village closed upon him, not a common barrier dropped across the road behind him, but he knew it to be another iron door in the series that was barred between him and England. The universal watchfulness so encompassed him, that if he had been taken in a net, or were being forwarded to his destination in a cage, he could not have felt his freedom more completely gone.

This universal watchfulness not only stopped him on the highway twenty times in a stage, but retarded his progress twenty times in a day, by riding after him and taking him back, riding before him and stopping him by anticipation, riding with him and keeping him in charge. He had been days upon his journey in France alone, when he went to bed tired out, in a little town on the high road, still a long way from Paris.

Nothing but the production of the afflicted Gabelle's letter from his prison of the Abbaye would have got him on so far. His difficulty at the guard-house in this small place had been such, that he felt his journey to have come to a crisis. And he was, therefore, as little surprised as a man could be, to find himself awakened at the small inn to which he had been remitted until morning, in the middle of the night.

Awakened by a timid local functionary and three armed patriots in rough red caps and with pipes in their mouths, who sat down on the bed.

"Emigrant," said the functionary, "I am going to send you on to Paris, under an escort."

"Citizen, I desire nothing more than to get to Paris, though I could dispense with the escort."

"Silence!" growled a red-cap, striking at the coverlet with the butt-end of his musket. "Peace, aristocrat!"

"It is as the good patriot says," observed the timid functionary. "You are an aristocrat, and must have an escort – and must pay for it."

"I have no choice," said Charles Darnay.

"Choice! Listen to him!" cried the same scowling red-cap. "As if it was not a favour to be protected from the lamp-iron!"

"It is always as the good patriot says," observed the functionary. "Rise and dress yourself, emigrant."

Darnay complied, and was taken back to the guard-house, where other patriots in rough red caps were smoking, drinking, and sleeping, by a watch-fire. Here he paid a heavy price for his escort, and hence he started with it on the wet, wet roads at three o'clock in the morning.

The escort were two mounted patriots in red caps and tri-coloured cockades, armed with national muskets and sabres, who rode one on either side of him.

The escorted governed his own horse, but a loose line was attached to his bridle, the end of which one of the patriots kept girded round his wrist. In this state they set forth with the sharp rain driving in their faces: clattering at a heavy dragoon trot over the uneven town pavement, and out upon the mire-deep roads. In this state they traversed without change, except of horses and pace, all the mire-deep leagues that lay between them and the capital.

They travelled in the night, halting an hour or two after daybreak, and lying by until the twilight fell. The escort were so wretchedly clothed, that they twisted straw round their bare legs, and thatched their ragged shoulders to keep the wet off. Apart from the personal discomfort of being so attended, and apart from such considerations of present danger as arose from one of the patriots being chronically drunk, and carrying his musket very recklessly, Charles Darnay did not allow the restraint that was laid upon him to awaken any serious fears in his breast; for, he reasoned with himself that it could have no reference to the merits of an individual case that was not yet stated, and of representations, confirmable by the prisoner in the Abbaye, that were not yet made.

But when they came to the town of Beauvais – which they did at eventide, when the streets were filled with people – he could not conceal from himself that the aspect of affairs was very alarming. An ominous crowd gathered to see him dismount of the posting-yard, and many voices called out loudly, “Down with the emigrant!”

He stopped in the act of swinging himself out of his saddle, and, resuming it as his safest place, said:

“Emigrant, my friends! Do you not see me here, in France, of my own will?”

“You are a cursed emigrant,” cried a farrier, making at him in a furious manner through the press, hammer in hand; “and you are a cursed aristocrat!”

The postmaster interposed himself between this man and the rider’s bridle (at which he was evidently making), and soothingly said, “Let him be; let him be! He will be judged at Paris.”

“Judged!” repeated the farrier, swinging his hammer. “Ay! and condemned as a traitor.” At this the crowd roared approval.

Checking the postmaster, who was for turning his horse's head to the yard (the drunken patriot sat composedly in his saddle looking on, with the line round his wrist), Darnay said, as soon as he could make his voice heard:

"Friends, you deceive yourselves, or you are deceived. I am not a traitor."

"He lies!" cried the smith. "He is a traitor since the decree. His life is forfeit to the people. His cursed life is not his own!"

At the instant when Darnay saw a rush in the eyes of the crowd, which another instant would have brought upon him, the postmaster turned his horse into the yard, the escort rode in close upon his horse's flanks, and the postmaster shut and barred the crazy double gates. The farrier struck a blow upon them with his hammer, and the crowd groaned; but, no more was done.

"What is this decree that the smith spoke of?" Darnay asked the postmaster, when he had thanked him, and stood beside him in the yard.

"Truly, a decree for selling the property of emigrants."

"When passed?"

"On the fourteenth."

"The day I left England!"

"Everybody says it is but one of several, and that there will be others – if there are not already – banishing all emigrants, and condemning all to death who return. That is what he meant when he said your life was not your own."

"But there are no such decrees yet?"

"What do I know!" said the postmaster, shrugging his shoulders; "there may be, or there will be. It is all the same. What would you have?"

They rested on some straw in a loft until the middle of the night, and then rode forward again when all the town was asleep. Among the many wild changes observable on familiar things which made this wild ride unreal, not the least was the seeming rarity of sleep. After long and lonely spurring over dreary roads, they would come to a cluster of poor cottages, not steeped in darkness, but all glittering with lights, and would find the people, in a ghostly manner in the dead of the night, circling hand in hand round a shrivelled tree of Liberty, or all drawn up together singing a Liberty song. Happily, however, there was sleep in Beauvais that night to help them out of it and they passed on once more into solitude and loneliness: jingling through the untimely cold and wet, among impoverished fields that had yielded no fruits of the earth that year, diversified by the blackened remains of burnt houses, and by the sudden emergence from ambuscade, and sharp reining up across their way, of patriot patrols on the watch on all the roads.

Daylight at last found them before the wall of Paris. The barrier was closed and strongly guarded when they rode up to it.

"Where are the papers of this prisoner?" demanded a resolute-looking man in authority, who was summoned out by the guard.

Naturally struck by the disagreeable word, Charles Darnay requested the speaker to take notice that he was a free traveller and French citizen, in charge of an escort which the disturbed state of the country had imposed upon him, and which he had paid for.

"Where," repeated the same personage, without taking any heed of him whatever, "are the papers of this prisoner?"

The drunken patriot had them in his cap, and produced them. Casting his eyes over Gabelle's letter, the same personage in authority showed some disorder and surprise, and looked at Darnay with a close attention.

He left escort and escorted without saying a word, however, and went into the guard-room; meanwhile, they sat upon their horses outside the gate. Looking about him while in this state of suspense, Charles Darnay observed that the gate was held by a mixed guard of soldiers and patriots, the latter far outnumbering the former; and that while ingress into the city for peasants' carts bringing in supplies, and for similar traffic and traffickers, was easy enough, egress, even for the homeliest people, was very difficult. A numerous medley of men and women, not to mention beasts and vehicles of various sorts, was waiting to issue forth; but, the previous identification was so strict, that they filtered through the barrier very slowly. Some of these people knew their turn for examination to be so far off, that they lay down on the ground to sleep or smoke, while others talked together, or loitered about. The red cap and tri-colour cockade were universal, both among men and women.

When he had sat in his saddle some half-hour, taking note of these things, Darnay found himself confronted by the same man in authority, who directed the guard to open the barrier. Then he delivered to the escort, drunk and sober, a receipt for the escorted, and requested him to dismount. He did so, and the two patriots, leading his tired horse, turned and rode away without entering the city.

He accompanied his conductor into a guard-room, smelling of common wine and tobacco, where certain soldiers and patriots, asleep and awake, drunk and sober, and in various neutral states between sleeping and waking, drunkenness and sobriety, were standing and lying about. The light in the guard-house, half derived from the waning oil-lamps of the night, and half from the overcast day, was in a correspondingly uncertain condition. Some registers were lying open on a desk, and an officer of a coarse, dark aspect, presided over these.

"Citizen Defarge," said he to Darnay's conductor, as he took a slip of paper to write on. "Is this the emigrant Evremonde?"

"This is the man."

"Your age, Evremonde?"

"Thirty-seven."

"Married, Evremonde?"

"Yes."

"Where married?"

"In England."

"Without doubt. Where is your wife, Evremonde?"

"In England."

"Without doubt. You are consigned, Evremonde, to the prison of La Force."

"Just Heaven!" exclaimed Darnay. "Under what law, and for what offence?"

The officer looked up from his slip of paper for a moment.

"We have new laws, Evremonde, and new offences, since you were here." He said it with a hard smile, and went on writing.

"I entreat you to observe that I have come here voluntarily, in response to that written appeal of a fellow-countryman which lies before you. I demand no more than the opportunity to do so without delay. Is not that my right?"

"Emigrants have no rights, Evremonde," was the stolid reply. The officer wrote until he had finished, read over to himself what he had written, sanded it, and handed it to Defarge, with the words "In secret."

Defarge motioned with the paper to the prisoner that he must accompany him. The prisoner obeyed, and a guard of two armed patriots attended them.

"Is it you," said Defarge, in a low voice, as they went down the guardhouse steps and turned into Paris, "who married the daughter of Doctor Manette, once a prisoner in the Bastille that is no more?"

"Yes," replied Darnay, looking at him with surprise.

"My name is Defarge, and I keep a wine-shop in the Quarter Saint Antoine. Possibly you have heard of me."

"My wife came to your house to reclaim her father? Yes!"

The word "wife" seemed to serve as a

gloomy reminder to Defarge, to say with sudden impatience, "In the name of that sharp female newly-born, and called La Guillotine, why did you come to France?"

"You heard me say why, a minute ago. Do you not believe it is the truth?"

"A bad truth for you," said Defarge, speaking with knitted brows, and looking straight before him.

"Indeed I am lost here. All here is so unprecedented, so changed, so sudden and unfair, that I am absolutely lost. Will you render me a little help?"

"None." Defarge spoke, always looking straight before him.

"Will you answer me a single question?"

"Perhaps. According to its nature. You can say what it is."

"In this prison that I am going to so unjustly, shall I have some free communication with the world outside?"

"You will see."

"I am not to be buried there, prejudged,

and without any means of presenting my case?"

"You will see. But, what then? Other people have been similarly buried in worse prisons, before now."

"But never by me, Citizen Defarge."

Defarge glanced darkly at him for answer, and walked on in a steady and set silence. The deeper he sank into this silence, the fainter hope there was – or so Darnay thought – of his softening in any slight degree. He, therefore, made haste to say:

"It is of the utmost importance to me (you know, Citizen, even better than I, of how much importance), that I should be able to communicate to Mr. Lorry of Tellson's Bank, an English gentleman who is now in Paris, the simple fact, without comment, that I have been thrown into the prison of La Force. Will you cause that to be done for me?"

"I will do," Defarge doggedly rejoined, "nothing for you. My duty is to my country and the People. I am the sworn servant of both, against you. I will do nothing for you."

Charles Darnay felt it hopeless to entreat him further, and his pride was touched besides. As they walked on in silence, he could not but see how used the people were to the spectacle of prisoners passing along the streets. The very children scarcely noticed him. A few passers turned their heads, and a few shook their fingers at him as an aristocrat; otherwise, that a man in good clothes should be going to prison, was no more remarkable than that a labourer in working clothes should be going to work. In one narrow, dark, and dirty street through which they passed, an excited orator, mounted on a stool, was addressing an excited audience on the crimes against the people, of the king and the royal family. The few words that he caught from this man's lips, first made it known to Charles Darnay that the king was in prison, and that the foreign ambassadors had one and all left Paris.

On the road (except at Beauvais) he had heard absolutely nothing. The escort and the universal watchfulness had completely isolated him.

That he had fallen among far greater dangers than those which had developed themselves when he left England, he of course knew now. That perils had thickened about him fast, and might thicken faster and faster yet, he of course knew now. He could not but admit to himself that he might not have made this journey, if he could have foreseen the events of a few days. And yet his misgivings were not so dark as, imagined by the light of this later time, they would appear. Troubled as the future was, it was the unknown future, and in its obscurity there was ignorant hope. The horrible massacre, days and nights long, which, within a few rounds of the clock, was to set a great mark of blood upon the blessed garnering time of harvest, was as far out of his knowledge as if it had been a hundred thousand years away. The “sharp female newly-born, and called La Guillotine,” was hardly known to him, or to the generality of people, by name. The frightful deeds that were to be soon done, were probably unimagined at that time in the brains of the doers. How could they have a place in the shadowy conceptions of a gentle mind?

Of unjust treatment in detention and hardship, and in cruel separation from his wife and child, he foreshadowed the likelihood, or the certainty; but, beyond this, he dreaded nothing distinctly. With this on his mind, which was enough to carry into a dreary prison courtyard, he arrived at the prison of La Force.

A man with a bloated face opened the strong wicket, to whom Defarge presented “The Emigrant Evremonde.”

“What the Devil! How many more of them!” exclaimed the man with the bloated face.

Defarge took his receipt without noticing the exclamation, and withdrew, with his two fellow-patriots.

"What the Devil, I say again!" exclaimed the gaoler, left with his wife. "How many more!"

The gaoler's wife, being provided with no answer to the question, merely replied, "One must have patience, my dear!" Three turnkeys who entered responsive to a bell she rang, echoed the sentiment, and one added, "For the love of Liberty;" which sounded in that place like an inappropriate conclusion.

The prison of La Force was a gloomy prison, dark and filthy, and with a horrible smell of foul sleep in it. Extraordinary how soon the noisome flavour of imprisoned sleep, becomes manifest in all such places that are ill cared for!

"In secret, too," grumbled the gaoler, looking at the written paper. "As if I was not already full to bursting!"

He stuck the paper on a file, in an ill-humour, and Charles Darnay awaited his further pleasure for half an hour: sometimes, pacing to and fro in the strong arched room: sometimes, resting on a stone seat: in either case detained to be imprinted on the memory of the chief and his subordinates.

"Come!" said the chief, at length taking up his keys, "come with me, emigrant."

Through the dismal prison twilight, his new charge accompanied him by corridor and staircase, many doors clanging and locking behind them, until they came into a large, low, vaulted chamber, crowded with prisoners of both sexes. The women were seated at a long table, reading and writing, knitting, sewing, and embroidering; the men were for the most part standing behind their chairs, or lingering up and down the room.

In the instinctive association of prisoners with shameful crime and disgrace, the new-comer recoiled from this company. But the crowning unreality of his long unreal ride, was, their all at once rising to receive him, with every refinement of manner known to the time, and with all the engaging graces and courtesies of life.

So strangely clouded were these refinements by the prison manners and gloom, so spectral did they become in the inappropriate squalor and misery through which they were seen, that Charles Darnay seemed to stand in a company of the dead. Ghosts all! The ghost of beauty, the ghost of stateliness, the ghost of elegance, the ghost of pride, the ghost of frivolity, the ghost of wit, the ghost of youth, the ghost of age, all waiting their dismissal from the desolate shore, all turning on him eyes that were changed by the death they had died in coming there.

It struck him motionless. The gaoler standing at his side, and the other gaolers moving about, who would have been well enough as to appearance in the ordinary exercise of their functions, looked so extravagantly coarse contrasted with sorrowing mothers and blooming daughters who were there – with the apparitions of the coquette, the young beauty, and the mature woman delicately bred – that the inversion of all experience and likelihood which the scene of shadows presented, was heightened to its utmost. Surely, ghosts all. Surely, the long unreal ride some progress of disease that had brought him to these gloomy shades!

"In the name of the assembled companions in misfortune," said a gentleman of courtly appearance and address, coming forward, "I have the honour of giving you welcome to La Force, and of condoling with you on the calamity that has brought you among us. May it soon terminate happily! It would be an impertinence elsewhere, but it is not so here, to ask your name and condition?"

Charles Darnay roused himself, and gave the required information, in words as suitable as he could find.

"But I hope," said the gentleman, following the chief gaoler with his eyes, who moved across the room, "that you are not in secret?"

"I do not understand the meaning of the term, but I have heard them say so."

"Ah, what a pity! We so much regret it! But take courage; several members of our society have been in secret, at first, and it has lasted but a short time." Then he added, raising his voice, "I grieve to inform the society – in secret."

There was a murmur of commiseration as Charles Darnay crossed the room to a grated door where the gaoler awaited him, and many voices – among which, the soft and compassionate voices of women were conspicuous – gave him good wishes and encouragement. He turned at the grated door, to render the thanks of his heart; it closed under the gaoler's hand; and the apparitions vanished from his sight forever.

The wicket opened on a stone staircase, leading upward. When they had ascended forty steps (the prisoner of half an hour already counted them), the gaoler opened a low black door, and they passed into a solitary cell. It struck cold and damp, but was not dark.

"Yours," said the gaoler.

"Why am I confined alone?"

"How do I know!"

"I can buy pen, ink, and paper?"

"Such are not my orders. You will be visited, and can ask then. At present, you may buy your food, and nothing more."

There were in the cell, a chair, a table, and a straw mattress. As the gaoler made a general inspection of these objects, and of the four walls, before going out, a wandering fancy wandered through the mind of the prisoner leaning against the wall opposite to him, that this gaoler was so unwholesomely bloated, both in face and person, as to look like a man who had been drowned and filled with water. When the gaoler was gone, he thought in the same wandering way, "Now am I left, as if I were dead." Stopping then, to look down at the mattress, he turned from it with a sick feeling, and thought, "And here in these crawling creatures is the first condition of the body after death."

"Five paces by four and a half, five paces by four and a half, five paces by four and a half." The prisoner walked to and fro in his cell, counting its measurement, and the roar of the city arose like muffled drums with a wild swell of voices added to them. "He made shoes, he made shoes, he made shoes." The prisoner counted the measurement again, and paced faster, to draw his mind with him from that latter repetition. "The ghosts that vanished when the wicket closed. There was one among them, the appearance of a lady dressed in black, who was leaning in the embrasure of a window, and she had a light shining upon her golden hair, and she looked like * * * * Let us ride on again, for God's sake, through the illuminated villages with the people all awake! * * * * He made shoes, he made shoes, he made shoes. * * * * Five paces by four and a half." With such scraps tossing and rolling upward from the depths of his mind, the prisoner walked faster and faster, obstinately counting and counting; and the roar of the city changed to this extent – that it still rolled in like muffled drums, but with the wail of voices that he knew, in the swell that rose above them.

CHAPTER TWO

The Grindstone

TELLSON'S BANK, established in the Saint Germain Quarter of Paris, was in a wing of a large house, approached by a courtyard and shut off from the street by a high wall and a strong gate. The house belonged to a great nobleman who had lived in it until he made a flight from the troubles, in his own cook's dress, and got across the borders. A mere beast of the chase flying from hunters, he was still in his metempsychosis no other than the same Monseigneur, the preparation of whose chocolate for whose lips had once occupied three strong men besides the cook in question.

Monseigneur gone, and the three strong men absolving themselves from the sin of having drawn his high wages, by being more than ready and willing to cut his throat on the altar of the dawning Republic one and indivisible of Liberty, Equality, Fraternity, or Death, Monseigneur's house had been first sequestrated, and then confiscated. For, all things moved so fast, and decree followed decree with that fierce precipitation, that now upon the third night of the autumn month of September, patriot emissaries of the law were in possession of Monseigneur's house, and had marked it with the tri-colour, and were drinking brandy in its state apartments.

A place of business in London like Tellson's place of business in Paris, would soon have driven the House out of its mind and into the Gazette. For, what would staid British responsibility and respectability have said to orange-trees in boxes in a Bank courtyard, and even to a Cupid over the counter? Yet such things were. Tellson's had whitewashed the Cupid, but he was still to be seen on the ceiling, in the coolest linen, aiming (as he very often does) at money from morning to night. Bankruptcy must inevitably have come of this young Pagan, in Lombard-street, London, and also of a curtained alcove in the rear of the immortal boy, and also of a looking-glass let into the wall, and also of clerks not at all old, who danced in public on the slightest provocation. Yet, a French Tellson's could get on with these things exceedingly well, and, as long as the times held together, no man had taken fright at them, and drawn out his money.

What money would be drawn out of Tellson's henceforth, and what would lie there, lost and forgotten; what plate and jewels would tarnish in Tellson's hiding-places, while the depositors rusted in prisons, and when they should have violently perished; how many accounts with Tellson's never to be balanced in this world, must be carried over into the next; no man could have said, that night, any more than Mr. Jarvis Lorry could, though he thought heavily of these questions. He sat by a newly-lighted wood fire (the blighted and unfruitful year was prematurely cold), and on his honest and courageous face there was a deeper shade than the pendent lamp could throw, or any object in the room distortedly reflect – a shade of horror.

He occupied rooms in the Bank, in his fidelity to the House of which he had grown to be a part, like strong root-ivy. It chanced that they derived a kind of security from the patriotic occupation of the main building, but the true-hearted old gentleman never calculated about that. All such circumstances were indifferent to him, so that he did his duty. On the opposite side of the courtyard, under a colonnade, was extensive standing – for carriages – where, indeed, some carriages of Monseigneur yet stood. Against two of the pillars were fastened two great flaring flambeaux, and in the light of these, standing out in the open air, was a large grindstone: a roughly mounted thing which appeared to have hurriedly been brought there from some neighbouring smithy, or other workshop. Rising and looking out of window at these harmless objects, Mr. Lorry shivered, and retired to his seat by the fire. He had opened, not only the glass window, but the lattice blind outside it, and he had closed both again, and he shivered through his frame.

From the streets beyond the high wall and the strong gate, there came the usual night hum of the city, with now and then an indescribable ring in it, weird and unearthly, as if some unwonted sounds of a terrible nature were going up to Heaven.

"Thank God," said Mr. Lorry, clasping his hands, "that no one near and dear to me is in this dreadful town to-night. May He have mercy on all who are in danger!"

Soon afterwards, the bell at the great gate sounded, and he thought, "They have come back!" and sat listening. But, there was no loud irruption into the courtyard, as he had expected, and he heard the gate clash again, and all was quiet.

The nervousness and dread that were upon him inspired that vague uneasiness respecting the Bank, which a great change would naturally awaken, with such feelings roused. It was well guarded, and he got up to go among the trusty people who were watching it, when his door suddenly opened, and two figures rushed in, at sight of which he fell back in amazement.

Lucie and her father! Lucie with her arms stretched out to him, and with that old look of earnestness so concentrated and intensified, that it seemed as though it had been stamped upon her face expressly to give force and power to it in this one passage of her life.

"What is this?" cried Mr. Lorry, breathless and confused. "What is the matter? Lucie! Manette! What has happened? What has brought you here? What is it?"

With the look fixed upon him, in her paleness and wildness, she panted out in his arms, imploringly, "O my dear friend! My husband!"

"Your husband, Lucie?"

"Charles."

"What of Charles?"

"Here.

"Here, in Paris?"

"Has been here some days – three or four – I don't know how many – I can't collect my thoughts. An errand of generosity brought him here unknown to us; he was stopped at the barrier, and sent to prison."

The old man uttered an irrepressible cry. Almost at the same moment, the bell of the great gate rang again, and a loud noise of feet and voices came pouring into the courtyard.

"What is that noise?" said the Doctor, turning towards the window.

"Don't look!" cried Mr. Lorry. "Don't look out! Manette, for your life, don't touch the blind!"

The Doctor turned, with his hand upon the fastening of the window, and said, with a cool, bold smile:

"My dear friend, I have a charmed life in this city. I have been a Bastille prisoner. There is no patriot in Paris – in Paris? In France – who, knowing me to have been a prisoner in the Bastille, would touch me, except to overwhelm me with embraces, or carry me in triumph. My old pain has given me a power that has brought us through the barrier, and gained us news of Charles there, and brought us here. I knew it would be so; I knew I could help Charles out of all danger; I told Lucie so. – What is that noise?"

His hand was again upon the window.

"Don't look!" cried Mr. Lorry, absolutely desperate. "No, Lucie, my dear, nor you!" He got his arm round her, and held her. "Don't be so terrified, my love. I solemnly swear to you that I know of no harm having happened to Charles; that I had no suspicion even of his being in this fatal place. What prison is he in?"

"La Force!"

"La Force! Lucie, my child, if ever you were brave and serviceable in your life – and you were always both – you will compose yourself now, to do exactly as I bid you; for more depends upon it than you can think, or I can say. There is no help for you in any action on your part to-night; you cannot possibly stir out. I say this, because what I must bid you to do for Charles's sake, is the hardest thing to do of all. You must instantly be obedient, still, and quiet. You must let me put you in a room at the back here. You must leave your father and me alone for two minutes, and as there are Life and Death in the world you must not delay."

"I will be submissive to you. I see in your face that you know I can do nothing else than this. I know you are true."

The old man kissed her, and hurried her into his room, and turned the key; then, came hurrying back to the Doctor, and opened the window and partly opened the blind, and put his hand upon the Doctor's arm, and looked out with him into the courtyard.

Looked out upon a throng of men and women: not enough in number, or near enough, to fill the courtyard: not more than forty or fifty in all. The people in possession of the house had let them in at the gate, and they had rushed in to work at the grindstone; it had evidently been set up there for their purpose, as in a convenient and retired spot.

But, such awful workers, and such awful work!

The grindstone had a double handle, and,

turning at it madly were two men, whose faces, as their long hair flapped back when the whirlings of the grindstone brought their faces up, were more horrible and cruel than the visages of the wildest savages in their most barbarous disguise. False eyebrows and false moustaches were stuck upon them, and their hideous countenances were all bloody and sweaty, and all awry with howling, and all staring and glaring with beastly excitement and want of sleep. As these ruffians turned and turned, their matted locks now flung forward over their eyes, now flung backward over their necks, some women held wine to their mouths that they might drink; and what with dropping blood, and what with dropping wine, and what with the stream of sparks struck out of the stone, all their wicked atmosphere seemed gore and fire. The eye could not detect one creature in the group free from the smear of blood. Shouldering one another to get next at the sharpening-stone, were men stripped to the waist, with the stain all over their limbs and bodies; men in all sorts of rags, with the stain upon those rags; men devilishly set off with spoils of women's lace and silk and ribbon, with the stain dyeing those trifles through and through. Hatchets, knives, bayonets, swords, all brought to be sharpened, were all red with it. Some of the hacked swords were tied to the wrists of those who carried them, with strips of linen and fragments of dress: ligatures various in kind, but all deep of the one colour. And as the frantic wielders of these weapons snatched them from the stream of sparks and tore away into the streets, the same red hue was red in their frenzied eyes; – eyes which any unbrutalised beholder would have given twenty years of life, to petrify with a well-directed gun.

All this was seen in a moment, as the vision of a drowning man, or of any human creature at any very great pass, could see a world if it were there. They drew back from the window, and the Doctor looked for explanation in his friend's ashy face.

"They are," Mr. Lorry whispered the words, glancing fearfully round at the locked room, "murdering the prisoners. If you are sure of what you say; if you really have the power you think you have – as I believe you have – make yourself known to these devils, and get taken to La Force. It may be too late, I don't know, but let it not be a minute later!"

Doctor Manette pressed his hand, hastened bareheaded out of the room, and was in the courtyard when Mr. Lorry regained the blind.

His streaming white hair, his remarkable face, and the impetuous confidence of his manner, as he put the weapons aside like water, carried him in an instant to the heart of the concourse at the stone. For a few moments there was a pause, and a hurry, and a murmur, and the unintelligible sound of his voice; and then Mr. Lorry saw him, surrounded by all, and in the midst of a line of twenty men long, all linked shoulder to shoulder, and hand to shoulder, hurried out with cries of – ”Live the Bastille prisoner! Help for the Bastille prisoner’s kindred in La Force! Room for the Bastille prisoner in front there! Save the prisoner Evremonde at La Force!” and a thousand answering shouts.

He closed the lattice again with a fluttering heart, closed the window and the curtain, hastened to Lucie, and told her that her father was assisted by the people, and gone in search of her husband. He found her child and Miss Pross with her; but, it never occurred to him to be surprised by their appearance until a long time afterwards, when he sat watching them in such quiet as the night knew.

Lucie had, by that time, fallen into a stupor on the floor at his feet, clinging to his hand. Miss Pross had laid the child down on his own bed, and her head had gradually fallen on the pillow beside her pretty charge. O the long, long night, with the moans of the poor wife! And O the long, long night, with no return of her father and no tidings!

Twice more in the darkness the bell at the great gate sounded, and the irruption was repeated, and the grindstone whirled and spluttered. “What is it?” cried Lucie, affrighted. “Hush! The soldiers’ swords are sharpened there,” said Mr. Lorry. “The place is national property now, and used as a kind of armoury, my love.”

Twice more in all; but, the last spell of work was feeble and fitful. Soon afterwards the day began to dawn, and he softly detached himself from the clasping hand, and cautiously looked out again. A man, so besmeared that he might have been a sorely wounded soldier creeping back to consciousness on a field of slain, was rising from the pavement by the side of the grindstone, and looking about him with a vacant air. Shortly, this worn-out murderer descried in the imperfect light one of the carriages of Monseigneur, and, staggering to that gorgeous vehicle, climbed in at the door, and shut himself up to take his rest on its dainty cushions.

The great grindstone, Earth, had turned when Mr. Lorry looked out again, and the sun was red on the courtyard. But, the lesser grindstone stood alone there in the calm morning air, with a red upon it that the sun had never given, and would never take away.

CHAPTER THREE

The Shadow

ONE OF THE first considerations which arose in the business mind of Mr. Lorry when business hours came round, was this: – that he had no right to imperil Tellson's by sheltering the wife of an emigrant prisoner under the Bank roof. His own possessions, safety, life, he would have hazarded for Lucie and her child, without a moment's demur; but the great trust he held was not his own, and as to that business charge he was a strict man of business.

At first, his mind reverted to Defarge, and he thought of finding out the wine-shop again and taking counsel with its master in reference to the safest dwelling-place in the distracted state of the city. But, the same consideration that suggested him, repudiated him; he lived in the most violent Quarter, and doubtless was influential there, and deep in its dangerous workings.

Noon coming, and the Doctor not returning, and every minute's delay tending to compromise Tellson's, Mr. Lorry advised with Lucie. She said that her father had spoken of hiring a lodging for a short term, in that Quarter, near the Banking-house. As there was no business objection to this, and as he foresaw that even if it were all well with Charles, and he were to be released, he could not hope to leave the city, Mr. Lorry went out in quest of such a lodging, and found a suitable one, high up in a removed by-street where the closed blinds in all the other windows of a high melancholy square of buildings marked deserted homes.

To this lodging he at once removed Lucie and her child, and Miss Pross: giving them what comfort he could, and much more than he had himself. He left Jerry with them, as a figure to fill a doorway that would bear considerable knocking on the head, and returned to his own occupations. A disturbed and doleful mind he brought to bear upon them, and slowly and heavily the day lagged on with him.

It wore itself out, and wore him out with it, until the Bank closed. He was again alone in his room of the previous night, considering what to do next, when he heard a foot upon the stair. In a few moments, a man stood in his presence, who, with a keenly observant look at him, addressed him by his name.

"Your servant," said Mr. Lorry. "Do you know me?"

He was a strongly made man with dark curling hair, from forty-five to fifty years of age. For answer he repeated, without any change of emphasis, the words:

"Do you know me?"

"I have seen you somewhere."

"Perhaps at my wine-shop?"

Much interested and agitated, Mr. Lorry said: "You come from Doctor Manette?"

"Yes. I come from Doctor Manette."

"And what says he? What does he send me?"

Defarge gave into his anxious hand, an open scrap of paper. It bore the words in the Doctor's writing:

"Charles is safe, but I cannot safely leave this place yet. I have obtained the favour that the bearer has a short note from Charles to his wife. Let the bearer see his wife."

It was dated from La Force, within an hour.

"Will you accompany me," said Mr. Lorry, joyfully relieved after reading this note aloud, "to where his wife resides?"

"Yes," returned Defarge.

Scarcely noticing as yet, in what a curiously reserved and mechanical way Defarge spoke, Mr. Lorry put on his hat and they went down into the courtyard. There, they found two women; one, knitting.

“Madame Defarge, surely!” said Mr. Lorry, who had left her in exactly the same attitude some seventeen years ago.

“It is she,” observed her husband.

“Does Madame go with us?” inquired Mr. Lorry, seeing that she moved as they moved.

“Yes. That she may be able to recognise the faces and know the persons. It is for their safety.”

Beginning to be struck by Defarge’s manner, Mr. Lorry looked dubiously at him, and led the way. Both the women followed; the second woman being The Vengeance.

They passed through the intervening streets as quickly as they might, ascended the staircase of the new domicile, were admitted by Jerry, and found Lucie weeping, alone. She was thrown into a transport by the tidings Mr. Lorry gave her of her husband, and clasped the hand that delivered his note – little thinking what it had been doing near him in the night, and might, but for a chance, have done to him.

"**Dearest**, – Take courage. I am well, and your father has influence around me. You cannot answer this. Kiss our child for me."

That was all the writing. It was so much, however, to her who received it, that she turned from Defarge to his wife, and kissed one of the hands that knitted. It was a passionate, loving, thankful, womanly action, but the hand made no response – dropped cold and heavy, and took to its knitting again.

There was something in its touch that gave Lucie a check. She stopped in the act of putting the note in her bosom, and, with her hands yet at her neck, looked terrified at Madame Defarge. Madame Defarge met the lifted eyebrows and forehead with a cold, impassive stare.

"My dear," said Mr. Lorry, striking in to explain; "there are frequent risings in the streets; and, although it is not likely they will ever trouble you, Madame Defarge wishes to see those whom she has the power to protect at such times, to the end that she may know them – that she may identify them. I believe," said Mr. Lorry, rather halting in his reassuring words, as the stony manner of all the three impressed itself upon him more and more, "I state the case, Citizen Defarge?"

Defarge looked gloomily at his wife, and gave no other answer than a gruff sound of acquiescence.

"You had better, Lucie," said Mr. Lorry, doing all he could to propitiate, by tone and manner, "have the dear child here, and our good Pross. Our good Pross, Defarge, is an English lady, and knows no French."

The lady in question, whose rooted conviction that she was more than a match for any foreigner, was not to be shaken by distress and, danger, appeared with folded arms, and observed in English to The Vengeance, whom her eyes first encountered, "Well, I am sure, Boldface! I hope **you** are pretty well!" She also bestowed a British cough on Madame Defarge; but, neither of the two took much heed of her.

"Is that his child?" said Madame Defarge, stopping in her work for the first time, and pointing her knitting-needle at little Lucie as if it were the finger of Fate.

"Yes, madame," answered Mr. Lorry; "this is our poor prisoner's darling daughter, and only child."

The shadow attendant on Madame Defarge and her party seemed to fall so threatening and dark on the child, that her mother instinctively kneeled on the ground beside her, and held her to her breast. The shadow attendant on Madame Defarge and her party seemed then to fall, threatening and dark, on both the mother and the child.

"It is enough, my husband," said Madame Defarge. "I have seen them. We may go."

But, the suppressed manner had enough of menace in it – not visible and presented, but indistinct and withheld – to alarm Lucie into saying, as she laid her appealing hand on Madame Defarge's dress:

"You will be good to my poor husband. You will do him no harm. You will help me to see him if you can?"

"Your husband is not my business here," returned Madame Defarge, looking down at her with perfect composure. "It is the daughter of your father who is my business here."

"For my sake, then, be merciful to my husband. For my child's sake! She will put her hands together and pray you to be merciful. We are more afraid of you than of these others."

Madame Defarge received it as a compliment, and looked at her husband. Defarge, who had been uneasily biting his thumb-nail and looking at her, collected his face into a sterner expression.

"What is it that your husband says in that little letter?" asked Madame Defarge, with a lowering smile. "Influence; he says something touching influence?"

"That my father," said Lucie, hurriedly taking the paper from her breast, but with her alarmed eyes on her questioner and not on it, "has much influence around him."

"Surely it will release him!" said Madame Defarge. "Let it do so."

"As a wife and mother," cried Lucie, most earnestly, "I implore you to have pity on me and not to exercise any power that you possess, against my innocent husband, but to use it in his behalf. O sister-woman, think of me. As a wife and mother!"

Madame Defarge looked, coldly as ever, at the suppliant, and said, turning to her friend The Vengeance:

"The wives and mothers we have been used to see, since we were as little as this child, and much less, have not been greatly considered? We have known **their** husbands and fathers laid in prison and kept from them, often enough? All our lives, we have seen our sister-women suffer, in themselves and in their children, poverty, nakedness, hunger, thirst, sickness, misery, oppression and neglect of all kinds?"

"We have seen nothing else," returned The Vengeance.

"We have borne this a long time," said Madame Defarge, turning her eyes again upon Lucie. "Judge you! Is it likely that the trouble of one wife and mother would be much to us now?"

She resumed her knitting and went out. The Vengeance followed. Defarge went last, and closed the door.

"Courage, my dear Lucie," said Mr. Lorry, as he raised her. "Courage, courage! So far all goes well with us – much, much better than it has of late gone with many poor souls. Cheer up, and have a thankful heart."

"I am not thankless, I hope, but that dreadful woman seems to throw a shadow on me and on all my hopes."

"Tut, tut!" said Mr. Lorry; "what is this despondency in the brave little breast? A shadow indeed! No substance in it, Lucie."

But the shadow of the manner of these Defarges was dark upon himself, for all that, and in his secret mind it troubled him greatly.

CHAPTER FOUR

Calm in Storm

DOCTOR MANETTE did not return until the morning of the fourth day of his absence. So much of what had happened in that dreadful time as could be kept from the knowledge of Lucie was so well concealed from her, that not until long afterwards, when France and she were far apart, did she know that eleven hundred defenceless prisoners of both sexes and all ages had been killed by the populace; that four days and nights had been darkened by this deed of horror; and that the air around her had been tainted by the slain. She only knew that there had been an attack upon the prisons, that all political prisoners had been in danger, and that some had been dragged out by the crowd and murdered.

To Mr. Lorry, the Doctor communicated under an injunction of secrecy on which he had no need to dwell, that the crowd had taken him through a scene of carnage to the prison of La Force. That, in the prison he had found a self-appointed Tribunal sitting, before which the prisoners were brought singly, and by which they were rapidly ordered to be put forth to be massacred, or to be released, or (in a few cases) to be sent back to their cells. That, presented by his conductors to this Tribunal, he had announced himself by name and profession as having been for eighteen years a secret and unaccused prisoner in the Bastille; that, one of the body so sitting in judgment had risen and identified him, and that this man was Defarge.

That, hereupon he had ascertained, through the registers on the table, that his son-in-law was among the living prisoners, and had pleaded hard to the Tribunal – of whom some members were asleep and some awake, some dirty with murder and some clean, some sober and some not – for his life and liberty. That, in the first frantic greetings lavished on himself as a notable sufferer under the overthrown system, it had been accorded to him to have Charles Darnay brought before the lawless Court, and examined. That, he seemed on the point of being at once released, when the tide in his favour met with some unexplained check (not intelligible to the Doctor), which led to a few words of secret conference. That, the man sitting as President had then informed Doctor Manette that the prisoner must remain in custody, but should, for his sake, be held inviolate in safe custody. That, immediately, on a signal, the prisoner was removed to the interior of the prison again; but, that he, the Doctor, had then so strongly pleaded for permission to remain and assure himself that his son-in-law was, through no malice or mischance, delivered to the concourse whose murderous yells outside the gate had often drowned the proceedings, that he had obtained the permission, and had remained in that Hall of Blood until the danger was over.

The sights he had seen there, with brief snatches of food and sleep by intervals, shall remain untold. The mad joy over the prisoners who were saved, had astounded him scarcely less than the mad ferocity against those who were cut to pieces. One prisoner there was, he said, who had been discharged into the street free, but at whom a mistaken savage had thrust a pike as he passed out. Being besought to go to him and dress the wound, the Doctor had passed out at the same gate, and had found him in the arms of a company of Samaritans, who were seated on the bodies of their victims. With an inconsistency as monstrous as anything in this awful nightmare, they had helped the healer, and tended the wounded man with the gentlest solicitude – had made a litter for him and escorted him carefully from the spot – had then caught up their weapons and plunged anew into a butchery so dreadful, that the Doctor had covered his eyes with his hands, and swooned away in the midst of it.

As Mr. Lorry received these confidences, and as he watched the face of his friend now sixty-two years of age, a misgiving arose within him that such dread experiences would revive the old danger.

But, he had never seen his friend in his present aspect: he had never at all known him in his present character. For the first time the Doctor felt, now, that his suffering was strength and power. For the first time he felt that in that sharp fire, he had slowly forged the iron which could break the prison door of his daughter's husband, and deliver him. "It all tended to a good end, my friend; it was not mere waste and ruin. As my beloved child was helpful in restoring me to myself, I will be helpful now in restoring the dearest part of herself to her; by the aid of Heaven I will do it!" Thus, Doctor Manette. And when Jarvis Lorry saw the kindled eyes, the resolute face, the calm strong look and bearing of the man whose life always seemed to him to have been stopped, like a clock, for so many years, and then set going again with an energy which had lain dormant during the cessation of its usefulness, he believed.

Greater things than the Doctor had at that time to contend with, would have yielded before his persevering purpose. While he kept himself in his place, as a physician, whose business was with all degrees of mankind, bond and free, rich and poor, bad and good, he used his personal influence so wisely, that he was soon the inspecting physician of three prisons, and among them of La Force. He could now assure Lucie that her husband was no longer confined alone, but was mixed with the general body of prisoners; he saw her husband weekly, and brought sweet messages to her, straight from his lips; sometimes her husband himself sent a letter to her (though never by the Doctor's hand), but she was not permitted to write to him: for, among the many wild suspicions of plots in the prisons, the wildest of all pointed at emigrants who were known to have made friends or permanent connections abroad.

This new life of the Doctor's was an anxious life, no doubt; still, the sagacious Mr. Lorry saw that there was a new sustaining pride in it. Nothing unbecoming tinged the pride; it was a natural and worthy one; but he observed it as a curiosity. The Doctor knew, that up to that time, his imprisonment had been associated in the minds of his daughter and his friend, with his personal affliction, deprivation, and weakness. Now that this was changed, and he knew himself to be invested through that old trial with forces to which they both looked for Charles's ultimate safety and deliverance, he became so far exalted by the change, that he took the lead and direction, and required them as the weak, to trust to him as the strong. The preceding relative positions of himself and Lucie were reversed, yet only as the liveliest gratitude and affection could reverse them, for he could have had no pride but in rendering some service to her who had rendered so much to him. "All curious to see," thought Mr. Lorry, in his amiably shrewd way, "but all natural and right; so, take the lead, my dear friend, and keep it; it couldn't be in better hands."

But, though the Doctor tried hard, and never ceased trying, to get Charles Darnay set at liberty, or at least to get him brought to trial, the public current of the time set too strong and fast for him. The new era began; the king was tried, doomed, and beheaded; the Republic of Liberty, Equality, Fraternity, or Death, declared for victory or death against the world in arms; the black flag waved night and day from the great towers of Notre Dame; three hundred thousand men, summoned to rise against the tyrants of the earth, rose from all the varying soils of France, as if the dragon's teeth had been sown broadcast, and had yielded fruit equally on hill and plain, on rock, in gravel, and alluvial mud, under the bright sky of the South and under the clouds of the North, in fell and forest, in the vineyards and the olive-grounds and among the cropped grass and the stubble of the corn, along the fruitful banks of the broad rivers, and in the sand of the sea-shore. What private solicitude could rear itself against the deluge of the Year One of Liberty – the deluge rising from below, not falling from above, and with the windows of Heaven shut, not opened!

There was no pause, no pity, no peace, no interval of relenting rest, no measurement of time. Though days and nights circled as regularly as when time was young, and the evening and morning were the first day, other count of time there was none. Hold of it was lost in the raging fever of a nation, as it is in the fever of one patient. Now, breaking the unnatural silence of a whole city, the executioner showed the people the head of the king – and now, it seemed almost in the same breath, the head of his fair wife which had had eight weary months of imprisoned widowhood and misery, to turn it grey.

And yet, observing the strange law of contradiction which obtains in all such cases, the time was long, while it flamed by so fast. A revolutionary tribunal in the capital, and forty or fifty thousand revolutionary committees all over the land; a law of the Suspected, which struck away all security for liberty or life, and delivered over any good and innocent person to any bad and guilty one; prisons gorged with people who had committed no offence, and could obtain no hearing; these things became the established order and nature of appointed things, and seemed to be ancient usage before they were many weeks old. Above all, one hideous figure grew as familiar as if it had been before the general gaze from the foundations of the world – the figure of the sharp female called La Guillotine.

It was the popular theme for jests; it was the best cure for headache, it infallibly prevented the hair from turning grey, it imparted a peculiar delicacy to the complexion, it was the National Razor which shaved close: who kissed La Guillotine, looked through the little window and sneezed into the sack. It was the sign of the regeneration of the human race. It superseded the Cross. Models of it were worn on breasts from which the Cross was discarded, and it was bowed down to and believed in where the Cross was denied.

It sheared off heads so many, that it, and the ground it most polluted, were a rotten red. It was taken to pieces, like a toy-puzzle for a young Devil, and was put together again when the occasion wanted it. It hushed the eloquent, struck down the powerful, abolished the beautiful and good. Twenty-two friends of high public mark, twenty-one living and one dead, it had lopped the heads off, in one morning, in as many minutes. The name of the strong man of Old Scripture had descended to the chief functionary who worked it; but, so armed, he was stronger than his namesake, and blinder, and tore away the gates of God's own Temple every day.

Among these terrors, and the brood belonging to them, the Doctor walked with a steady head: confident in his power, cautiously persistent in his end, never doubting that he would save Lucie's husband at last. Yet the current of the time swept by, so strong and deep, and carried the time away so fiercely, that Charles had lain in prison one year and three months when the Doctor was thus steady and confident. So much more wicked and distracted had the Revolution grown in that December month, that the rivers of the South were encumbered with the bodies of the violently drowned by night, and prisoners were shot in lines and squares under the southern wintry sun. Still, the Doctor walked among the terrors with a steady head. No man better known than he, in Paris at that day; no man in a stranger situation. Silent, humane, indispensable in hospital and prison, using his art equally among assassins and victims, he was a man apart. In the exercise of his skill, the appearance and the story of the Bastille Captive removed him from all other men. He was not suspected or brought in question, any more than if he had indeed been recalled to life some eighteen years before, or were a Spirit moving among mortals.

CHAPTER FIVE

The Wood-Sawyer

ONE YEAR and three months. During all that time Lucie was never sure, from hour to hour, but that the Guillotine would strike off her husband's head next day. Every day, through the stony streets, the tumbrils now jolted heavily, filled with Condemned. Lovely girls; bright women, brown-haired, black-haired, and grey; youths; stalwart men and old; gentle born and peasant born; all red wine for La Guillotine, all daily brought into light from the dark cellars of the loathsome prisons, and carried to her through the streets to slake her devouring thirst. Liberty, equality, fraternity, or death; – the last, much the easiest to bestow, O Guillotine!

If the suddenness of her calamity, and the whirling wheels of the time, had stunned the Doctor's daughter into awaiting the result in idle despair, it would but have been with her as it was with many. But, from the hour when she had taken the white head to her fresh young bosom in the garret of Saint Antoine, she had been true to her duties. She was truest to them in the season of trial, as all the quietly loyal and good will always be.

As soon as they were established in their new residence, and her father had entered on the routine of his avocations, she arranged the little household as exactly as if her husband had been there. Everything had its appointed place and its appointed time. Little Lucie she taught, as regularly, as if they had all been united in their English home. The slight devices with which she cheated herself into the show of a belief that they would soon be reunited – the little preparations for his speedy return, the setting aside of his chair and his books – these, and the solemn prayer at night for one dear prisoner especially, among the many unhappy souls in prison and the shadow of death – were almost the only outspoken reliefs of her heavy mind.

She did not greatly alter in appearance. The plain dark dresses, akin to mourning dresses, which she and her child wore, were as neat and as well attended to as the brighter clothes of happy days. She lost her colour, and the old and intent expression was a constant, not an occasional, thing; otherwise, she remained very pretty and comely. Sometimes, at night on kissing her father, she would burst into the grief she had repressed all day, and would say that her sole reliance, under Heaven, was on him.

He always resolutely answered: “Nothing can happen to him without my knowledge, and I know that I can save him, Lucie.”

They had not made the round of their changed life many weeks, when her father said to her, on coming home one evening:

“My dear, there is an upper window in the prison, to which Charles can sometimes gain access at three in the afternoon. When he can get to it – which depends on many uncertainties and incidents – he might see you in the street, he thinks, if you stood in a certain place that I can show you. But you will not be able to see him, my poor child, and even if you could, it would be unsafe for you to make a sign of recognition.”

“O show me the place, my father, and I will go there every day.”

From that time, in all weathers, she waited there two hours. As the clock struck two, she was there, and at four she turned resignedly away. When it was not too wet or inclement for her child to be with her, they went together; at other times she was alone; but, she never missed a single day.

It was the dark and dirty corner of a small winding street. The hovel of a cutter of wood into lengths for burning, was the only house at that end; all else was wall. On the third day of her being there, he noticed her.

"Good day, citizeness."

"Good day, citizen."

This mode of address was now prescribed by decree. It had been established voluntarily some time ago, among the more thorough patriots; but, was now law for everybody.

"Walking here again, citizeness?"

"You see me, citizen!"

The wood-sawyer, who was a little man with a redundancy of gesture (he had once been a mender of roads), cast a glance at the prison, pointed at the prison, and putting his ten fingers before his face to represent bars, peeped through them jocosely.

"But it's not my business," said he. And went on sawing his wood.

Next day he was looking out for her, and accosted her the moment she appeared.

"What? Walking here again, citizeness?"

"Yes, citizen."

"Ah! A child too! Your mother, is it not, my little citizeness?"

"Do I say yes, mamma?" whispered little Lucie, drawing close to her.

"Yes, dearest."

"Yes, citizen."

"Ah! But it's not my business. My work is my business. See my saw! I call it my Little Guillotine. La, la, la; La, la, la! And off his head comes!"

The billet fell as he spoke, and he threw it into a basket.

"I call myself the Samson of the firewood guillotine. See here again! Loo, loo, loo; Loo, loo, loo! And off **her** head comes! Now, a child. Tickle, tickle; Pickle, pickle! And off **its** head comes. All the family!"

Lucie shuddered as he threw two more billets into his basket, but it was impossible to be there while the wood-sawyer was at work, and not be in his sight. Thenceforth, to secure his good will, she always spoke to him first, and often gave him drink-money, which he readily received.

He was an inquisitive fellow, and sometimes when she had quite forgotten him in gazing at the prison roof and grates, and in lifting her heart up to her husband, she would come to herself to find him looking at her, with his knee on his bench and his saw stopped in its work. “But it’s not my business!” he would generally say at those times, and would briskly fall to his sawing again.

In all weathers, in the snow and frost of winter, in the bitter winds of spring, in the hot sunshine of summer, in the rains of autumn, and again in the snow and frost of winter, Lucie passed two hours of every day at this place; and every day on leaving it, she kissed the prison wall. Her husband saw her (so she learned from her father) it might be once in five or six times: it might be twice or thrice running: it might be, not for a week or a fortnight together. It was enough that he could and did see her when the chances served, and on that possibility she would have waited out the day, seven days a week.

These occupations brought her round to the December month, wherein her father walked among the terrors with a steady head. On a lightly-snowing afternoon she arrived at the usual corner. It was a day of some wild rejoicing, and a festival. She had seen the houses, as she came along, decorated with little pikes, and with little red caps stuck upon them; also, with tricoloured ribbons; also, with the standard inscription (tricoloured letters were the favourite), Republic One and Indivisible. Liberty, Equality, Fraternity, or Death!

The miserable shop of the wood-sawyer was so small, that its whole surface furnished very indifferent space for this legend. He had got somebody to scrawl it up for him, however, who had squeezed Death in with most inappropriate difficulty. On his house-top, he displayed pike and cap, as a good citizen must, and in a window he had stationed his saw inscribed as his "Little Sainte Guillotine" – for the great sharp female was by that time popularly canonised. His shop was shut and he was not there, which was a relief to Lucie, and left her quite alone.

But, he was not far off, for presently she heard a troubled movement and a shouting coming along, which filled her with fear. A moment afterwards, and a throng of people came pouring round the corner by the prison wall, in the midst of whom was the wood-sawyer hand in hand with The Vengeance. There could not be fewer than five hundred people, and they were dancing like five thousand demons. There was no other music than their own singing. They danced to the popular Revolution song, keeping a ferocious time that was like a gnashing of teeth in unison. Men and women danced together, women danced together, men danced together, as hazard had brought them together. At first, they were a mere storm of coarse red caps and coarse woollen rags; but, as they filled the place, and stopped to dance about Lucie, some ghastly apparition of a dance-figure gone raving mad arose among them. They advanced, retreated, struck at one another's hands, clutched at one another's heads, spun round alone, caught one another and spun round in pairs, until many of them dropped. While those were down, the rest linked hand in hand, and all spun round together: then the ring broke, and in separate rings of two and four they turned and turned until they all stopped at once, began again, struck, clutched, and tore, and then reversed the spin, and all spun round another way. Suddenly they stopped again, paused, struck out the time afresh, formed into lines the width of the public way, and, with their heads low down and their hands high up, swooped screaming off. No fight could have been half so terrible as this dance. It was so emphatically a fallen sport – a something, once innocent, delivered over to all devilry – a healthy pastime changed into a means of angering the blood, bewildering the senses, and steeling the heart. Such grace as was visible in it, made it the uglier, showing how warped and perverted all things good by nature were become. The maidenly bosom bared to this, the pretty almost-child's head thus distracted, the delicate foot mincing in this slough of blood and dirt, were types of the disjointed time.

This was the Carmagnole. As it passed, leaving Lucie frightened and bewildered in the doorway of the wood-sawyer's house, the feathery snow fell as quietly and lay as white and soft, as if it had never been.

"O my father!" for he stood before her when she lifted up the eyes she had momentarily darkened with her hand; “such a cruel, bad sight.”

“I know, my dear, I know. I have seen it many times. Don’t be frightened! Not one of them would harm you.”

“I am not frightened for myself, my father. But when I think of my husband, and the mercies of these people – ”

“We will set him above their mercies very soon. I left him climbing to the window, and I came to tell you. There is no one here to see. You may kiss your hand towards that highest shelving roof.”

“I do so, father, and I send him my Soul with it!”

“You cannot see him, my poor dear?”

“No, father,” said Lucie, yearning and weeping as she kissed her hand, “no.”

A footstep in the snow. Madame Defarge. “I salute you, citizeness,” from the Doctor. “I salute you, citizen.” This in passing. Nothing more. Madame Defarge gone, like a shadow over the white road.

"Give me your arm, my love. Pass from here with an air of cheerfulness and courage, for his sake. That was well done;" they had left the spot; "it shall not be in vain. Charles is summoned for to-morrow."

"For to-morrow!"

"There is no time to lose. I am well prepared, but there are precautions to be taken, that could not be taken until he was actually summoned before the Tribunal. He has not received the notice yet, but I know that he will presently be summoned for to-morrow, and removed to the Conciergerie; I have timely information. You are not afraid?"

She could scarcely answer, "I trust in you."

"Do so, implicitly. Your suspense is nearly ended, my darling; he shall be restored to you within a few hours; I have encompassed him with every protection. I must see Lorry."

He stopped. There was a heavy lumbering of wheels within hearing. They both knew too well what it meant. One. Two. Three. Three tumbrils faring away with their dread loads over the hushing snow.

"I must see Lorry," the Doctor repeated, turning her another way.

The staunch old gentleman was still in his trust; had never left it. He and his books were in frequent requisition as to property confiscated and made national. What he could save for the owners, he saved. No better man living to hold fast by what Tellson's had in keeping, and to hold his peace.

A murky red and yellow sky, and a rising mist from the Seine, denoted the approach of darkness. It was almost dark when they arrived at the Bank. The stately residence of Monseigneur was altogether blighted and deserted. Above a heap of dust and ashes in the court, ran the letters: National Property. Republic One and Indivisible. Liberty, Equality, Fraternity, or Death!

Who could that be with Mr. Lorry – the owner of the riding-coat upon the chair – who must not be seen? From whom newly arrived, did he come out, agitated and surprised, to take his favourite in his arms? To whom did he appear to repeat her faltering words, when, raising his voice and turning his head towards the door of the room from which he had issued, he said: “Removed to the Conciergerie, and summoned for to-morrow?”

CHAPTER SIX

Triumph

THE DREAD tribunal of five Judges, Public Prosecutor, and determined Jury, sat every day. Their lists went forth every evening, and were read out by the gaolers of the various prisons to their prisoners. The standard gaoler-joke was, "Come out and listen to the Evening Paper, you inside there!"

"Charles Evremonde, called Darnay!"

So at last began the Evening Paper at La

Force.

When a name was called, its owner stepped apart into a spot reserved for those who were announced as being thus fatally recorded. Charles Evremonde, called Darnay, had reason to know the usage; he had seen hundreds pass away so.

His bloated gaoler, who wore spectacles to read with, glanced over them to assure himself that he had taken his place, and went through the list, making a similar short pause at each name. There were twenty-three names, but only twenty were responded to; for one of the prisoners so summoned had died in gaol and been forgotten, and two had already been guillotined and forgotten. The list was read, in the vaulted chamber where Darnay had seen the associated prisoners on the night of his arrival. Every one of those had perished in the massacre; every human creature he had since cared for and parted with, had died on the scaffold.

There were hurried words of farewell and

kindness, but the parting was soon over. It was the incident of every day, and the society of La Force were engaged in the preparation of some games of forfeits and a little concert, for that evening. They crowded to the grates and shed tears there; but, twenty places in the projected entertainments had to be refilled, and the time was, at best, short to the lock-up hour, when the common rooms and corridors would be delivered over to the great dogs who kept watch there through the night. The prisoners were far from insensible or unfeeling; their ways arose out of the condition of the time. Similarly, though with a subtle difference, a species of fervour or intoxication, known, without doubt, to have led some persons to brave the guillotine unnecessarily, and to die by it, was not mere boastfulness, but a wild infection of the wildly shaken public mind. In seasons of pestilence, some of us will have a secret attraction to the disease – a terrible passing inclination to die of it. And all of us have like wonders hidden in our breasts, only needing circumstances to evoke them.

The passage to the Conciergerie was short and dark; the night in its vermin-haunted cells was long and cold. Next day, fifteen prisoners were put to the bar before Charles Darnay's name was called. All the fifteen were condemned, and the trials of the whole occupied an hour and a half.

"Charles Evremonde, called Darnay," was at length arraigned.

His judges sat upon the Bench in feathered hats; but the rough red cap and tricoloured cockade was the head-dress otherwise prevailing. Looking at the Jury and the turbulent audience, he might have thought that the usual order of things was reversed, and that the felons were trying the honest men. The lowest, cruelest, and worst populace of a city, never without its quantity of low, cruel, and bad, were the directing spirits of the scene: noisily commenting, applauding, disapproving, anticipating, and precipitating the result, without a check. Of the men, the greater part were armed in various ways; of the women, some wore knives, some daggers, some ate and drank as they looked on, many knitted. Among these last, was one, with a spare piece of knitting under her arm as she worked. She was in a front row, by the side of a man whom he had never seen since his arrival at the Barrier, but whom he directly remembered as Defarge. He noticed that she once or twice whispered in his ear, and that she seemed to be his wife; but, what he most noticed in the two figures was, that although they were posted as close to himself as they could be, they never looked towards him. They seemed to be waiting for something with a dogged determination, and they looked at the Jury, but at nothing else. Under the President sat Doctor Manette, in his usual quiet dress. As well as the prisoner could see, he and Mr. Lorry were the only men there, unconnected with the Tribunal, who wore their usual clothes, and had not assumed the coarse garb of the Carmagnole.

Charles Evremonde, called Darnay, was accused by the public prosecutor as an emigrant, whose life was forfeit to the Republic, under the decree which banished all emigrants on pain of Death. It was nothing that the decree bore date since his return to France. There he was, and there was the decree; he had been taken in France, and his head was demanded.

"Take off his head!" cried the audience. "An enemy to the Republic!"

The President rang his bell to silence those cries, and asked the prisoner whether it was not true that he had lived many years in England?

Undoubtedly it was.

Was he not an emigrant then? What did he call himself?

Not an emigrant, he hoped, within the sense and spirit of the law.

Why not? the President desired to know.

Because he had voluntarily relinquished

a title that was distasteful to him, and a station that was distasteful to him, and had left his country – he submitted before the word emigrant in the present acceptation by the Tribunal was in use – to live by his own industry in England, rather than on the industry of the overladen people of France.

What proof had he of this?

He handed in the names of two witnesses; Theophile Gabelle, and Alexandre Manette.

But he had married in England? the President reminded him.

True, but not an English woman.

A citizeness of France?

Yes. By birth.

Her name and family?

"Lucie Manette, only daughter of Doctor Manette, the good physician who sits there."

This answer had a happy effect upon the audience. Cries in exaltation of the well-known good physician rent the hall. So capriciously were the people moved, that tears immediately rolled down several ferocious countenances which had been glaring at the prisoner a moment before, as if with impatience to pluck him out into the streets and kill him.

On these few steps of his dangerous way, Charles Darnay had set his foot according to Doctor Manette's reiterated instructions. The same cautious counsel directed every step that lay before him, and had prepared every inch of his road.

The President asked, why had he returned to France when he did, and not sooner?

He had not returned sooner, he replied, simply because he had no means of living in France, save those he had resigned; whereas, in England, he lived by giving instruction in the French language and literature. He had returned when he did, on the pressing and written entreaty of a French citizen, who represented that his life was endangered by his absence. He had come back, to save a citizen's life, and to bear his testimony, at whatever personal hazard, to the truth. Was that criminal in the eyes of the Republic?

The populace cried enthusiastically, “No!” and the President rang his bell to quiet them. Which it did not, for they continued to cry “No!” until they left off, of their own will.

The President required the name of that citizen. The accused explained that the citizen was his first witness. He also referred with confidence to the citizen’s letter, which had been taken from him at the Barrier, but which he did not doubt would be found among the papers then before the President.

The Doctor had taken care that it should be there – had assured him that it would be there – and at this stage of the proceedings it was produced and read. Citizen Gabelle was called to confirm it, and did so. Citizen Gabelle hinted, with infinite delicacy and politeness, that in the pressure of business imposed on the Tribunal by the multitude of enemies of the Republic with which it had to deal, he had been slightly overlooked in his prison of the Abbaye – in fact, had rather passed out of the Tribunal's patriotic remembrance – until three days ago; when he had been summoned before it, and had been set at liberty on the Jury's declaring themselves satisfied that the accusation against him was answered, as to himself, by the surrender of the citizen Evremonde, called Darnay.

Doctor Manette was next questioned. His high personal popularity, and the clearness of his answers, made a great impression; but, as he proceeded, as he showed that the Accused was his first friend on his release from his long imprisonment; that, the accused had remained in England, always faithful and devoted to his daughter and himself in their exile; that, so far from being in favour with the Aristocrat government there, he had actually been tried for his life by it, as the foe of England and friend of the United States – as he brought these circumstances into view, with the greatest discretion and with the straightforward force of truth and earnestness, the Jury and the populace became one. At last, when he appealed by name to Monsieur Lorry, an English gentleman then and there present, who, like himself, had been a witness on that English trial and could corroborate his account of it, the Jury declared that they had heard enough, and that they were ready with their votes if the President were content to receive them.

At every vote (the Jurymen voted aloud and individually), the populace set up a shout of applause. All the voices were in the prisoner's favour, and the President declared him free.

Then, began one of those extraordinary scenes with which the populace sometimes gratified their fickleness, or their better impulses towards generosity and mercy, or which they regarded as some set-off against their swollen account of cruel rage. No man can decide now to which of these motives such extraordinary scenes were referable; it is probable, to a blending of all the three, with the second predominating. No sooner was the acquittal pronounced, than tears were shed as freely as blood at another time, and such fraternal embraces were bestowed upon the prisoner by as many of both sexes as could rush at him, that after his long and unwholesome confinement he was in danger of fainting from exhaustion; none the less because he knew very well, that the very same people, carried by another current, would have rushed at him with the very same intensity, to rend him to pieces and strew him over the streets.

His removal, to make way for other accused persons who were to be tried, rescued him from these caresses for the moment. Five were to be tried together, next, as enemies of the Republic, forasmuch as they had not assisted it by word or deed. So quick was the Tribunal to compensate itself and the nation for a chance lost, that these five came down to him before he left the place, condemned to die within twenty-four hours. The first of them told him so, with the customary prison sign of Death – a raised finger – and they all added in words, “Long live the Republic!”

The five had had, it is true, no audience to lengthen their proceedings, for when he and Doctor Manette emerged from the gate, there was a great crowd about it, in which there seemed to be every face he had seen in Court – except two, for which he looked in vain. On his coming out, the concourse made at him anew, weeping, embracing, and shouting, all by turns and all together, until the very tide of the river on the bank of which the mad scene was acted, seemed to run mad, like the people on the shore.

They put him into a great chair they had among them, and which they had taken either out of the Court itself, or one of its rooms or passages. Over the chair they had thrown a red flag, and to the back of it they had bound a pike with a red cap on its top. In this car of triumph, not even the Doctor's entreaties could prevent his being carried to his home on men's shoulders, with a confused sea of red caps heaving about him, and casting up to sight from the stormy deep such wrecks of faces, that he more than once misdoubted his mind being in confusion, and that he was in the tumbril on his way to the Guillotine.

In wild dreamlike procession, embracing whom they met and pointing him out, they carried him on. Reddening the snowy streets with the prevailing Republican colour, in winding and tramping through them, as they had reddened them below the snow with a deeper dye, they carried him thus into the courtyard of the building where he lived. Her father had gone on before, to prepare her, and when her husband stood upon his feet, she dropped insensible in his arms.

As he held her to his heart and turned her beautiful head between his face and the brawling crowd, so that his tears and her lips might come together unseen, a few of the people fell to dancing. Instantly, all the rest fell to dancing, and the courtyard overflowed with the Carmagnole. Then, they elevated into the vacant chair a young woman from the crowd to be carried as the Goddess of Liberty, and then swelling and overflowing out into the adjacent streets, and along the river's bank, and over the bridge, the Carmagnole absorbed them every one and whirled them away.

After grasping the Doctor's hand, as he stood victorious and proud before him; after grasping the hand of Mr. Lorry, who came panting in breathless from his struggle against the waterspout of the Carmagnole; after kissing little Lucie, who was lifted up to clasp her arms round his neck; and after embracing the ever zealous and faithful Pross who lifted her; he took his wife in his arms, and carried her up to their rooms.

"Lucie! My own! I am safe."

"O dearest Charles, let me thank God for this on my knees as I have prayed to Him."

They all reverently bowed their heads and hearts. When she was again in his arms, he said to her:

"And now speak to your father, dearest. No other man in all this France could have done what he has done for me."

She laid her head upon her father's breast, as she had laid his poor head on her own breast, long, long ago. He was happy in the return he had made her, he was recompensed for his suffering, he was proud of his strength. "You must not be weak, my darling," he remonstrated; "don't tremble so. I have saved him."

CHAPTER SEVEN

A Knock at the Door

"I HAVE saved him." It was not another of the dreams in which he had often come back; he was really here. And yet his wife trembled, and a vague but heavy fear was upon her.

All the air round was so thick and dark, the people were so passionately revengeful and fitful, the innocent were so constantly put to death on vague suspicion and black malice, it was so impossible to forget that many as blameless as her husband and as dear to others as he was to her, every day shared the fate from which he had been clutched, that her heart could not be as lightened of its load as she felt it ought to be. The shadows of the wintry afternoon were beginning to fall, and even now the dreadful carts were rolling through the streets. Her mind pursued them, looking for him among the Condemned; and then she clung closer to his real presence and trembled more.

Her father, cheering her, showed a compassionate superiority to this woman's weakness, which was wonderful to see. No garret, no shoemaking, no One Hundred and Five, North Tower, now! He had accomplished the task he had set himself, his promise was redeemed, he had saved Charles. Let them all lean upon him.

Their housekeeping was of a very frugal kind: not only because that was the safest way of life, involving the least offence to the people, but because they were not rich, and Charles, throughout his imprisonment, had had to pay heavily for his bad food, and for his guard, and towards the living of the poorer prisoners. Partly on this account, and partly to avoid a domestic spy, they kept no servant; the citizen and citizeness who acted as porters at the courtyard gate, rendered them occasional service; and Jerry (almost wholly transferred to them by Mr. Lorry) had become their daily retainer, and had his bed there every night.

It was an ordinance of the Republic One and Indivisible of Liberty, Equality, Fraternity, or Death, that on the door or doorpost of every house, the name of every inmate must be legibly inscribed in letters of a certain size, at a certain convenient height from the ground. Mr. Jerry Cruncher's name, therefore, duly embellished the doorpost down below; and, as the afternoon shadows deepened, the owner of that name himself appeared, from overlooking a painter whom Doctor Manette had employed to add to the list the name of Charles Evremonde, called Darnay.

In the universal fear and distrust that darkened the time, all the usual harmless ways of life were changed. In the Doctor's little household, as in very many others, the articles of daily consumption that were wanted were purchased every evening, in small quantities and at various small shops. To avoid attracting notice, and to give as little occasion as possible for talk and envy, was the general desire.

For some months past, Miss Pross and Mr. Cruncher had discharged the office of purveyors; the former carrying the money; the latter, the basket. Every afternoon at about the time when the public lamps were lighted, they fared forth on this duty, and made and brought home such purchases as were needful. Although Miss Pross, through her long association with a French family, might have known as much of their language as of her own, if she had had a mind, she had no mind in that direction; consequently she knew no more of that "nonsense" (as she was pleased to call it) than Mr. Cruncher did. So her manner of marketing was to plump a noun-substantive at the head of a shopkeeper without any introduction in the nature of an article, and, if it happened not to be the name of the thing she wanted, to look round for that thing, lay hold of it, and hold on by it until the bargain was concluded. She always made a bargain for it, by holding up, as a statement of its just price, one finger less than the merchant held up, whatever his number might be.

"Now, Mr. Cruncher," said Miss Pross, whose eyes were red with felicity; "if you are ready, I am."

Jerry hoarsely professed himself at Miss Pross's service. He had worn all his rust off long ago, but nothing would file his spiky head down.

"There's all manner of things wanted," said Miss Pross, "and we shall have a precious time of it. We want wine, among the rest. Nice toasts these Redheads will be drinking, wherever we buy it."

"It will be much the same to your knowledge, miss, I should think," retorted Jerry, "whether they drink your health or the Old Un's."

"Who's he?" said Miss Pross.

Mr. Cruncher, with some diffidence, explained himself as meaning "Old Nick's."

"Ha!" said Miss Pross, "it doesn't need an interpreter to explain the meaning of these creatures. They have but one, and it's Midnight Murder, and Mischief."

"Hush, dear! Pray, pray, be cautious!" cried Lucie.

"Yes, yes, yes, I'll be cautious," said Miss Pross; "but I may say among ourselves, that I do hope there will be no oniony and tobaccoey smotherings in the form of embracings all round, going on in the streets. Now, Ladybird, never you stir from that fire till I come back! Take care of the dear husband you have recovered, and don't move your pretty head from his shoulder as you have it now, till you see me again! May I ask a question, Doctor Manette, before I go?"

"I think you may take that liberty," the Doctor answered, smiling.

"For gracious sake, don't talk about Liberty; we have quite enough of that," said Miss Pross.

"Hush, dear! Again?" Lucie remonstrated.

"Well, my sweet," said Miss Pross, nodding her head emphatically, "the short and the long of it is, that I am a subject of His Most Gracious Majesty King George the Third;" Miss Pross curtseyed at the name; "and as such, my maxim is, Confound their politics, Frustrate their knavish tricks, On him our hopes we fix, God save the King!"

Mr. Cruncher, in an access of loyalty, growlingly repeated the words after Miss Pross, like somebody at church.

"I am glad you have so much of the Englishman in you, though I wish you had never taken that cold in your voice," said

Miss Pross, approvingly. "But the question, Doctor Manette. Is there" – it was the good creature's way to affect to make light of anything that was a great anxiety with them all, and to come at it in this chance manner – "is there any prospect yet, of our getting out of this place?"

"I fear not yet. It would be dangerous for Charles yet."

"Heigh-ho-hum!" said Miss Pross, cheerfully repressing a sigh as she glanced at her darling's golden hair in the light of the fire, "then we must have patience and wait: that's all. We must hold up our heads and fight low, as my brother Solomon used to say. Now, Mr. Cruncher! – Don't you move, Ladybird!"

They went out, leaving Lucie, and her husband, her father, and the child, by a bright fire. Mr. Lorry was expected back presently from the Banking House. Miss Pross had lighted the lamp, but had put it aside in a corner, that they might enjoy the fire-light undisturbed. Little Lucie sat by her grandfather with her hands clasped through his arm: and he, in a tone not rising much above a whisper, began to tell her a story of a great and powerful Fairy who had opened a prison-wall and let out a captive who had once done the Fairy a service. All was subdued and quiet, and Lucie was more at ease than she had been.

"What is that?" she cried, all at once.

"My dear!" said her father, stopping in his story, and laying his hand on hers, "command yourself. What a disordered state you are in! The least thing – nothing – startles you! **You**, your father's daughter!"

"I thought, my father," said Lucie, excusing herself, with a pale face and in a faltering voice, "that I heard strange feet upon the stairs."

"My love, the staircase is as still as Death."

As he said the word, a blow was struck upon the door.

"Oh father, father. What can this be! Hide

Charles. Save him!"

"My child," said the Doctor, rising, and laying his hand upon her shoulder, "I **have** saved him. What weakness is this, my dear! Let me go to the door."

He took the lamp in his hand, crossed the two intervening outer rooms, and opened it. A rude clattering of feet over the floor, and four rough men in red caps, armed with sabres and pistols, entered the room.

"The Citizen Evremonde, called Darnay," said the first.

"Who seeks him?" answered Darnay.

"I seek him. We seek him. I know you, Evremonde; I saw you before the Tribunal to-day. You are again the prisoner of the Republic."

The four surrounded him, where he stood with his wife and child clinging to him.

"Tell me how and why am I again a prisoner?"

"It is enough that you return straight to the Conciergerie, and will know to-morrow. You are summoned for to-morrow."

Doctor Manette, whom this visitation had so turned into stone, that he stood with the lamp in his hand, as if he were a statue made to hold it, moved after these words were spoken, put the lamp down, and confronting the speaker, and taking him, not ungently, by the loose front of his red woollen shirt, said:

"You know him, you have said. Do you know me?"

"Yes, I know you, Citizen Doctor."

"We all know you, Citizen Doctor," said the other three.

He looked abstractedly from one to another, and said, in a lower voice, after a pause:

"Will you answer his question to me then? How does this happen?"

"Citizen Doctor," said the first, reluctantly, "he has been denounced to the Section of Saint Antoine. This citizen," pointing out the second who had entered, "is from Saint

Antoine."

The citizen here indicated nodded his head, and added:

"He is accused by Saint Antoine."

"Of what?" asked the Doctor.

"Citizen Doctor," said the first, with his former reluctance, "ask no more. If the Republic demands sacrifices from you, without doubt you as a good patriot will be happy to make them. The Republic goes before all. The People is supreme. Evremonde, we are pressed."

"One word," the Doctor entreated. "Will you tell me who denounced him?"

"It is against rule," answered the first; "but you can ask Him of Saint Antoine here."

The Doctor turned his eyes upon that man. Who moved uneasily on his feet, rubbed his beard a little, and at length said:

"Well! Truly it is against rule. But he is denounced – and gravely – by the Citizen and Citizeness Defarge. And by one other."

"What other?"

"Do **you** ask, Citizen Doctor?"

"Yes."

"Then," said he of Saint Antoine, with a strange look, "you will be answered to-morrow. Now, I am dumb!"

CHAPTER EIGHT

A Hand at Cards

HAPPILY UNCONSCIOUS of the new calamity at home, Miss Pross threaded her way along the narrow streets and crossed the river by the bridge of the Pont-Neuf, reckoning in her mind the number of indispensable purchases she had to make. Mr. Cruncher, with the basket, walked at her side. They both looked to the right and to the left into most of the shops they passed, had a wary eye for all gregarious assemblages of people, and turned out of their road to avoid any very excited group of talkers. It was a raw evening, and the misty river, blurred to the eye with blazing lights and to the ear with harsh noises, showed where the barges were stationed in which the smiths worked, making guns for the Army of the Republic. Woe to the man who played tricks with **that** Army, or got undeserved promotion in it! Better for him that his beard had never grown, for the National Razor shaved him close.

Having purchased a few small articles of grocery, and a measure of oil for the lamp, Miss Pross bethought herself of the wine they wanted. After peeping into several wine-shops, she stopped at the sign of the Good Republican Brutus of Antiquity, not far from the National Palace, once (and twice) the Tuileries, where the aspect of things rather took her fancy. It had a quieter look than any other place of the same description they had passed, and, though red with patriotic caps, was not so red as the rest. Sounding Mr. Cruncher, and finding him of her opinion, Miss Pross resorted to the Good Republican Brutus of Antiquity, attended by her cavalier.

Slightly observant of the smoky lights; of the people, pipe in mouth, playing with limp cards and yellow dominoes; of the one bare-breasted, bare-armed, soot-begrimed workman reading a journal aloud, and of the others listening to him; of the weapons worn, or laid aside to be resumed; of the two or three customers fallen forward asleep, who in the popular high-shouldered shaggy black spencer looked, in that attitude, like slumbering bears or dogs; the two outlandish customers approached the counter, and showed what they wanted.

As their wine was measuring out, a man parted from another man in a corner, and rose to depart. In going, he had to face Miss Pross. No sooner did he face her, than Miss

Pross uttered a scream, and clapped her hands.

In a moment, the whole company were on their feet. That somebody was assassinated by somebody vindicating a difference of opinion was the likeliest occurrence. Everybody looked to see somebody fall, but only saw a man and a woman standing staring at each other; the man with all the outward aspect of a Frenchman and a thorough Republican; the woman, evidently English.

What was said in this disappointing anti-climax, by the disciples of the Good Republican Brutus of Antiquity, except that it was something very voluble and loud, would have been as so much Hebrew or Chaldean to Miss Pross and her protector, though they had been all ears. But, they had no ears for anything in their surprise. For, it must be recorded, that not only was Miss Pross lost in amazement and agitation, but, Mr. Cruncher – though it seemed on his own separate and individual account – was in a state of the greatest wonder.

"What is the matter?" said the man who had caused Miss Pross to scream; speaking in a vexed, abrupt voice (though in a low tone), and in English.

"Oh, Solomon, dear Solomon!" cried Miss Pross, clapping her hands again. "After not setting eyes upon you or hearing of you for so long a time, do I find you here!"

"Don't call me Solomon. Do you want to be the death of me?" asked the man, in a furtive, frightened way.

"Brother, brother!" cried Miss Pross, bursting into tears. "Have I ever been so hard with you that you ask me such a cruel question?"

"Then hold your meddlesome tongue," said Solomon, "and come out, if you want to speak to me. Pay for your wine, and come out. Who's this man?"

Miss Pross, shaking her loving and dejected head at her by no means affectionate brother, said through her tears, "Mr. Cruncher."

"Let him come out too," said Solomon. "Does he think me a ghost?"

Apparently, Mr. Cruncher did, to judge from his looks. He said not a word, however, and Miss Pross, exploring the depths of her reticule through her tears with great difficulty paid for her wine. As she did so, Solomon turned to the followers of the Good Republican Brutus of Antiquity, and offered a few words of explanation in the French language, which caused them all to relapse into their former places and pursuits.

"Now," said Solomon, stopping at the dark street corner, "what do you want?"

"How dreadfully unkind in a brother nothing has ever turned my love away from!" cried Miss Pross, "to give me such a greeting, and show me no affection."

"There. Confound it! There," said Solomon, making a dab at Miss Pross's lips with his own. "Now are you content?"

Miss Pross only shook her head and wept

in silence.

"If you expect me to be surprised," said her brother Solomon, "I am not surprised; I knew you were here; I know of most people who are here. If you really don't want to endanger my existence – which I half believe you do – go your ways as soon as possible, and let me go mine. I am busy. I am an official."

"My English brother Solomon," mourned Miss Pross, casting up her tear-fraught eyes, "that had the makings in him of one of the best and greatest of men in his native country, an official among foreigners, and such foreigners! I would almost sooner have seen the dear boy lying in his – "

"I said so!" cried her brother, interrupting. "I knew it. You want to be the death of me. I shall be rendered Suspected, by my own sister. Just as I am getting on!"

"The gracious and merciful Heavens forbid!" cried Miss Pross. "Far rather would I never see you again, dear Solomon, though

I have ever loved you truly, and ever shall. Say but one affectionate word to me, and tell me there is nothing angry or estranged between us, and I will detain you no longer."

Good Miss Pross! As if the estrangement between them had come of any culpability of hers. As if Mr. Lorry had not known it for a fact, years ago, in the quiet corner in Soho, that this precious brother had spent her money and left her!

He was saying the affectionate word, however, with a far more grudging condescension and patronage than he could have shown if their relative merits and positions had been reversed (which is invariably the case, all the world over), when Mr. Cruncher, touching him on the shoulder, hoarsely and unexpectedly interposed with the following singular question:

"I say! Might I ask the favour? As to whether your name is John Solomon, or Solomon John?"

The official turned towards him with sudden

distrust. He had not previously uttered a word.

"Come!" said Mr. Cruncher. "Speak out, you know." (Which, by the way, was more than he could do himself.) "John Solomon, or Solomon John? She calls you Solomon, and she must know, being your sister. And I know you're John, you know. Which of the two goes first? And regarding that name of Pross, likewise. That warn't your name over the water."

"What do you mean?"

"Well, I don't know all I mean, for I can't call to mind what your name was, over the water."

"No?"

"No. But I'll swear it was a name of two syllables."

"Indeed?"

"Yes. T'other one's was one syllable. I know you. You was a spy – witness at the Bailey. What, in the name of the Father of Lies, own father to yourself, was you called at that time?"

"Barsad," said another voice, striking in.

"That's the name for a thousand pound!" cried Jerry.

The speaker who struck in, was Sydney Carton. He had his hands behind him under the skirts of his riding-coat, and he stood at Mr. Cruncher's elbow as negligently as he might have stood at the Old Bailey itself.

"Don't be alarmed, my dear Miss Pross. I arrived at Mr. Lorry's, to his surprise, yesterday evening; we agreed that I would not present myself elsewhere until all was well, or unless I could be useful; I present myself here, to beg a little talk with your brother. I wish you had a better employed brother than Mr. Barsad. I wish for your sake Mr. Barsad was not a Sheep of the Prisons."

Sheep was a cant word of the time for a spy, under the gaolers. The spy, who was pale, turned paler, and asked him how he dared –

"I'll tell you," said Sydney. "I lighted on you, Mr. Barsad, coming out of the prison of the Conciergerie while I was contemplating the walls, an hour or more ago. You have a face to be remembered, and I remember faces well. Made curious by seeing you in that connection, and having a reason, to which you are no stranger, for associating you with the misfortunes of a friend now very unfortunate, I walked in your direction. I walked into the wine-shop here, close after you, and sat near you. I had no difficulty in deducing from your unreserved conversation, and the rumour openly going about among your admirers, the nature of your calling. And gradually, what I had done at random, seemed to shape itself into a purpose, Mr. Barsad."

"What purpose?" the spy asked.

"It would be troublesome, and might be dangerous, to explain in the street. Could you favour me, in confidence, with some minutes of your company – at the office of

Tellson's Bank, for instance?"

"Under a threat?"

"Oh! Did I say that?"

"Then, why should I go there?"

"Really, Mr. Barsad, I can't say, if you can't."

"Do you mean that you won't say, sir?" the spy irresolutely asked.

"You apprehend me very clearly, Mr. Barsad. I won't."

Carton's negligent recklessness of manner came powerfully in aid of his quickness and skill, in such a business as he had in his secret mind, and with such a man as he had to do with. His practised eye saw it, and made the most of it.

"Now, I told you so," said the spy, casting a reproachful look at his sister; "if any trouble comes of this, it's your doing."

"Come, come, Mr. Barsad!" exclaimed Sydney. "Don't be ungrateful. But for my great respect for your sister, I might not have led up so pleasantly to a little proposal that

I wish to make for our mutual satisfaction. Do you go with me to the Bank?"

"I'll hear what you have got to say. Yes, I'll go with you."

"I propose that we first conduct your sister safely to the corner of her own street. Let me take your arm, Miss Pross. This is not a good city, at this time, for you to be out in, unprotected; and as your escort knows Mr. Barsad, I will invite him to Mr. Lorry's with us. Are we ready? Come then!"

Miss Pross recalled soon afterwards, and to the end of her life remembered, that as she pressed her hands on Sydney's arm and looked up in his face, imploring him to do no hurt to Solomon, there was a braced purpose in the arm and a kind of inspiration in the eyes, which not only contradicted his light manner, but changed and raised the man. She was too much occupied then with fears for the brother who so little deserved her affection, and with Sydney's friendly reassurances, adequately to heed what she observed.

They left her at the corner of the street, and Carton led the way to Mr. Lorry's, which was within a few minutes' walk. John Barsad, or Solomon Pross, walked at his side.

Mr. Lorry had just finished his dinner, and was sitting before a cheery little log or two of fire – perhaps looking into their blaze for the picture of that younger elderly gentleman from Tellson's, who had looked into the red coals at the Royal George at Dover, now a good many years ago. He turned his head as they entered, and showed the surprise with which he saw a stranger.

"Miss Pross's brother, sir," said Sydney. "Mr. Barsad."

"Barsad?" repeated the old gentleman, "Barsad? I have an association with the name – and with the face."

"I told you you had a remarkable face, Mr. Barsad," observed Carton, coolly. "Pray sit down."

As he took a chair himself, he supplied the

link that Mr. Lorry wanted, by saying to him with a frown, "Witness at that trial." Mr. Lorry immediately remembered, and regarded his new visitor with an undisguised look of abhorrence.

"Mr. Barsad has been recognised by Miss Pross as the affectionate brother you have heard of," said Sydney, "and has acknowledged the relationship. I pass to worse news. Darnay has been arrested again."

Struck with consternation, the old gentleman exclaimed, "What do you tell me! I left him safe and free within these two hours, and am about to return to him!"

"Arrested for all that. When was it done, Mr. Barsad?"

"Just now, if at all."

"Mr. Barsad is the best authority possible, sir," said Sydney, "and I have it from Mr. Barsad's communication to a friend and brother Sheep over a bottle of wine, that the arrest has taken place. He left the messengers at the gate, and saw them admitted by the porter. There is no earthly doubt that he is retaken."

Mr. Lorry's business eye read in the speaker's face that it was loss of time to dwell upon the point. Confused, but sensible that something might depend on his presence of mind, he commanded himself, and was silently attentive.

"Now, I trust," said Sydney to him, "that the name and influence of Doctor Manette may stand him in as good stead to-morrow – you said he would be before the Tribunal again to-morrow, Mr. Barsad? – "

"Yes; I believe so."

" – In as good stead to-morrow as to-day. But it may not be so. I own to you, I am shaken, Mr. Lorry, by Doctor Manette's not having had the power to prevent this arrest."

"He may not have known of it beforehand," said Mr. Lorry.

"But that very circumstance would be alarming, when we remember how identified he is with his son-in-law."

"That's true," Mr. Lorry acknowledged, with his troubled hand at his chin, and his troubled eyes on Carton.

"In short," said Sydney, "this is a desperate time, when desperate games are played for desperate stakes. Let the Doctor play the winning game; I will play the losing one. No man's life here is worth purchase. Any one carried home by the people to-day, may be condemned tomorrow. Now, the stake I have resolved to play for, in case of the worst, is a friend in the Conciergerie. And the friend I purpose to myself to win, is Mr. Barsad."

"You need have good cards, sir," said the spy.

"I'll run them over. I'll see what I hold, – Mr. Lorry, you know what a brute I am; I wish you'd give me a little brandy."

It was put before him, and he drank off a glassful – drank off another glassful – pushed the bottle thoughtfully away.

"Mr. Barsad," he went on, in the tone of one who really was looking over a hand at cards: "Sheep of the prisons, emissary of Republican committees, now turnkey, now prisoner, always spy and secret informer, so much the more valuable here for being English that an Englishman is less open to suspicion of subornation in those characters than a Frenchman, represents himself to his employers under a false name. That's a very good card. Mr. Barsad, now in the employ of the republican French government, was formerly in the employ of the aristocratic English government, the enemy of France and freedom. That's an excellent card. Inference clear as day in this region of suspicion, that Mr. Barsad, still in the pay of the aristocratic English government, is the spy of Pitt, the treacherous foe of the Republic crouching in its bosom, the English traitor and agent of all mischief so much spoken of and so difficult to find. That's a card not to be beaten. Have you followed my hand, Mr. Barsad?"

"Not to understand your play," returned the spy, somewhat uneasily.

"I play my Ace, Denunciation of Mr. Barsad to the nearest Section Committee. Look over your hand, Mr. Barsad, and see what you have. Don't hurry."

He drew the bottle near, poured out another glassful of brandy, and drank it off. He saw that the spy was fearful of his drinking himself into a fit state for the immediate denunciation of him. Seeing it, he poured out and drank another glassful.

"Look over your hand carefully, Mr. Barsad. Take time."

It was a poorer hand than he suspected. Mr. Barsad saw losing cards in it that Sydney Carton knew nothing of. Thrown out of his honourable employment in England, through too much unsuccessful hard swearing there – not because he was not wanted there; our English reasons for vaunting our superiority to secrecy and spies are of very modern date – he knew that he had crossed the Channel, and accepted service in France: first, as a tempter and an eavesdropper among his own countrymen there: gradually, as a tempter and an eavesdropper among the natives. He knew that under the overthrown government he had been a spy upon Saint Antoine and Defarge's wine-shop; had received from the watchful police such heads of information concerning Doctor Manette's imprisonment, release, and history, as should serve him for an introduction to familiar conversation with the Defarges; and tried them on Madame Defarge, and had broken down with them signally. He always remembered with fear and trembling, that that terrible woman had knitted when he talked with her, and had looked ominously at him as her fingers moved. He had since seen her, in the Section of Saint Antoine, over and over again produce her knitted registers, and denounce people whose lives the guillotine then surely swallowed up. He knew, as every one employed as he was did, that he was never safe; that flight was impossible; that he was tied fast under the shadow of the axe; and that in spite of his utmost tergiversation and treachery in furtherance of the reigning terror, a word might bring it down upon him. Once denounced, and on such grave grounds as had just now been suggested to his mind, he foresaw that the dreadful woman of whose unrelenting character he had seen many proofs, would produce against him that fatal register, and would quash his last chance of life. Besides that all secret men are men soon terrified, here were surely cards enough of one black suit, to justify the holder in growing rather livid as he turned them over.

"You scarcely seem to like your hand," said Sydney, with the greatest composure. "Do you play?"

"I think, sir," said the spy, in the meanest manner, as he turned to Mr. Lorry, "I may appeal to a gentleman of your years and benevolence, to put it to this other gentleman, so much your junior, whether he can under any circumstances reconcile it to his station to play that Ace of which he has spoken. I admit that I am a spy, and that it is considered a discreditable station – though it must be filled by somebody; but this gentleman is no spy, and why should he so demean himself as to make himself one?"

"I play my Ace, Mr. Barsad," said Carton, taking the answer on himself, and looking at his watch, "without any scruple, in a very few minutes."

"I should have hoped, gentlemen both," said the spy, always striving to hook Mr. Lorry into the discussion, "that your respect for my sister – "

"I could not better testify my respect for your sister than by finally relieving her of her brother," said Sydney Carton.

"You think not, sir?"

"I have thoroughly made up my mind about it."

The smooth manner of the spy, curiously in dissonance with his ostentatiously rough dress, and probably with his usual demeanour, received such a check from the inscrutability of Carton, – who was a mystery to wiser and honester men than he, – that it faltered here and failed him. While he was at a loss, Carton said, resuming his former air of contemplating cards:

"And indeed, now I think again, I have a strong impression that I have another good card here, not yet enumerated. That friend and fellow-Sheep, who spoke of himself as pasturing in the country prisons; who was he?"

"French. You don't know him," said the spy, quickly.

"French, eh?" repeated Carton, musing, and not appearing to notice him at all, though he echoed his word. "Well; he may be."

"Is, I assure you," said the spy; "though it's not important."

"Though it's not important," repeated Carton, in the same mechanical way – "though it's not important – No, it's not important. No. Yet I know the face."

"I think not. I am sure not. It can't be," said the spy.

"It-can't-be," muttered Sydney Carton, retrospectively, and idling his glass (which fortunately was a small one) again. "Can't-be. Spoke good French. Yet like a foreigner, I thought?"

"Provincial," said the spy.

"No. Foreign!" cried Carton, striking his open hand on the table, as a light broke clearly on his mind. "Cly! Disguised, but the same man. We had that man before us at the Old Bailey."

"Now, there you are hasty, sir," said Barsad, with a smile that gave his aquiline nose an extra inclination to one side; "there you really give me an advantage over you. Cly (who

I will unreservedly admit, at this distance of time, was a partner of mine) has been dead several years. I attended him in his last illness. He was buried in London, at the church of Saint Pancras-in-the-Fields. His unpopularity with the blackguard multitude at the moment prevented my following his remains, but I helped to lay him in his coffin."

Here, Mr. Lorry became aware, from where he sat, of a most remarkable goblin shadow on the wall. Tracing it to its source, he discovered it to be caused by a sudden extraordinary rising and stiffening of all the risen and stiff hair on Mr. Cruncher's head.

"Let us be reasonable," said the spy, "and let us be fair. To show you how mistaken you are, and what an unfounded assumption yours is, I will lay before you a certificate of Cly's burial, which I happened to have carried in my pocket-book," with a hurried hand he produced and opened it, "ever since. There it is. Oh, look at it, look at it! You may take it in your hand; it's no forgery."

Here, Mr. Lorry perceived the reflection on the wall to elongate, and Mr. Cruncher rose and stepped forward. His hair could not have been more violently on end, if it had been that moment dressed by the Cow with the crumpled horn in the house that Jack built.

Unseen by the spy, Mr. Cruncher stood at his side, and touched him on the shoulder like a ghostly bailiff.

"That there Roger Cly, master," said Mr. Cruncher, with a taciturn and iron-bound visage. "So **you** put him in his coffin?"

"I did."

"Who took him out of it?"

Barsad leaned back in his chair, and stammered, "What do you mean?"

"I mean," said Mr. Cruncher, "that he warn't never in it. No! Not he! I'll have my head took off, if he was ever in it."

The spy looked round at the two gentlemen; they both looked in unspeakable astonishment at Jerry.

"I tell you," said Jerry, "that you buried paving-stones and earth in that there coffin. Don't go and tell me that you buried Cly. It was a take in. Me and two more knows it."

"How do you know it?"

"What's that to you? Ecod!" growled Mr. Cruncher, "it's you I have got a old grudge again, is it, with your shameful impositions upon tradesmen! I'd catch hold of your throat and choke you for half a guinea."

Sydney Carton, who, with Mr. Lorry, had been lost in amazement at this turn of the business, here requested Mr. Cruncher to moderate and explain himself.

"At another time, sir," he returned, evasively, "the present time is ill-conwenient for explainin'. What I stand to, is, that he knows well wot that there Cly was never in that there coffin. Let him say he was, in so much as a word of one syllable, and I'll either catch hold of his throat and choke him for half a guinea;" Mr. Cruncher dwelt upon this as quite a liberal offer; "or I'll out and announce him."

"Humph! I see one thing," said Carton. "I hold another card, Mr. Barsad. Impossible, here in raging Paris, with Suspicion filling the air, for you to outlive denunciation, when you are in communication with another aristocratic spy of the same antecedents as yourself, who, moreover, has the mystery about him of having feigned death and come to life again! A plot in the prisons, of the foreigner against the Republic. A strong card – a certain Guillotine card! Do you play?"

"No!" returned the spy. "I throw up. I confess that we were so unpopular with the outrageous mob, that I only got away from England at the risk of being ducked to death, and that Cly was so ferreted up and down, that he never would have got away at all but for that sham. Though how this man knows it was a sham, is a wonder of wonders to me."

"Never you trouble your head about this man," retorted the contentious Mr.

Cruncher; “you’ll have trouble enough with giving your attention to that gentleman. And look here! Once more!” – Mr. Cruncher could not be restrained from making rather an ostentatious parade of his liberality – ”I’d catch hold of your throat and choke you for half a guinea.”

The Sheep of the prisons turned from him to Sydney Carton, and said, with more decision, “It has come to a point. I go on duty soon, and can’t overstay my time. You told me you had a proposal; what is it? Now, it is of no use asking too much of me. Ask me to do anything in my office, putting my head in great extra danger, and I had better trust my life to the chances of a refusal than the chances of consent. In short, I should make that choice. You talk of desperation. We are all desperate here. Remember! I may denounce you if I think proper, and I can swear my way through stone walls, and so can others. Now, what do you want with me?”

"Not very much. You are a turnkey at the Conciergerie?"

"I tell you once for all, there is no such thing as an escape possible," said the spy, firmly.

"Why need you tell me what I have not asked? You are a turnkey at the Conciergerie?"

"I am sometimes."

"You can be when you choose?"

"I can pass in and out when I choose."

Sydney Carton filled another glass with brandy, poured it slowly out upon the hearth, and watched it as it dropped. It being all spent, he said, rising:

"So far, we have spoken before these two, because it was as well that the merits of the cards should not rest solely between you and me. Come into the dark room here, and let us have one final word alone."

CHAPTER NINE

The Game Made

WHILE SYDNEY Carton and the Sheep of the prisons were in the adjoining dark room, speaking so low that not a sound was heard, Mr. Lorry looked at Jerry in considerable doubt and mistrust. That honest tradesman's manner of receiving the look, did not inspire confidence; he changed the leg on which he rested, as often as if he had fifty of those limbs, and were trying them all; he examined his finger-nails with a very questionable closeness of attention; and whenever Mr. Lorry's eye caught his, he was taken with that peculiar kind of short cough requiring the hollow of a hand before it, which is seldom, if ever, known to be an infirmity attendant on perfect openness of character.

"Jerry," said Mr. Lorry. "Come here."

Mr. Cruncher came forward sideways, with one of his shoulders in advance of him.

"What have you been, besides a messenger?"

After some cogitation, accompanied with an intent look at his patron, Mr. Cruncher conceived the luminous idea of replying, "Agicultooral character."

"My mind misgives me much," said Mr. Lorry, angrily shaking a forefinger at him, "that you have used the respectable and great house of Tellson's as a blind, and that you have had an unlawful occupation of an infamous description. If you have, don't expect me to befriend you when you get back to England. If you have, don't expect me to keep your secret. Tellson's shall not be imposed upon."

"I hope, sir," pleaded the abashed Mr. Cruncher, "that a gentleman like yourself wot I've had the honour of odd jobbing till I'm grey at it, would think twice about harming of me, even if it wos so – I don't say it is, but even if it wos. And which it is to be took into account that if it wos, it wouldn't, even then, be all o' one side. There'd be two sides to it. There might be medical doctors at the present hour, a picking up their guineas where a honest tradesman don't pick up his fardens – fardens! no, nor yet his half fardens – half fardens! no, nor yet his quarter – a banking away like smoke at Tellson's, and a cocking their medical eyes at that tradesman on the sly, a going in and going out to their own carriages – ah! equally like smoke, if not more so. Well, that 'ud be imposing, too, on Tellson's. For you cannot sarse the goose and not the gander. And here's Mrs. Cruncher, or leastways wos in the Old England times, and would be to-morrow, if cause given, a floppin' again the business to that degree as is ruinating – stark ruinating! Whereas them medical doctors' wives don't flop – catch 'em at it! Or, if they flop, their floppings goes in favour of more patients, and how can you rightly have one without t'other? Then, wot with undertakers, and wot with parish clerks, and wot with sextons, and wot with private watchmen (all awaricious and all in it), a man wouldn't get much by it, even if it wos so. And wot little a man did get, would never prosper with him, Mr. Lorry. He'd never have no good of it; he'd want all along to be out of the line, if he, could see his way out, being once in – even if it wos so."

"Ugh!" cried Mr. Lorry, rather relenting, nevertheless, "I am shocked at the sight of you."

"Now, what I would humbly offer to you,

sir," pursued Mr. Cruncher, "even if it wos so, which I don't say it is – "

"Don't prevaricate," said Mr. Lorry.

"No, I will **not**, sir," returned Mr. Crunches as if nothing were further from his thoughts or practice – "which I don't say it is – wot I would humbly offer to you, sir, would be this. Upon that there stool, at that there Bar, sets that there boy of mine, brought up and growed up to be a man, wot will errand you, message you, general-light-job you, till your heels is where your head is, if such should be your wishes. If it wos so, which I still don't say it is (for I will not prewaricate to you, sir), let that there boy keep his father's place, and take care of his mother; don't blow upon that boy's father – do not do it, sir – and let that father go into the line of the reg'lar diggin', and make amends for what he would have undug – if it wos so – by diggin' of 'em in with a will, and with conwictions respectin' the futur' keepin' of 'em safe. That, Mr. Lorry," said Mr. Cruncher, wiping his forehead with his arm, as an announcement that he had arrived at the peroration of his discourse, "is wot I would respectfully offer to you, sir. A man don't see all this here a goin' on dreadful round him, in the way of Subjects without heads, dear me, plentiful enough fur to bring the price down to porterage and hardly that, without havin' his serious thoughts of things. And these here would be mine, if it wos so, entreatin' of you fur to bear in mind that wot I said just now, I up and said in the good cause when I might have kep' it back."

"That at least is true," said Mr. Lorry. "Say no more now. It may be that I shall yet stand your friend, if you deserve it, and repent in action – not in words. I want no more words."

Mr. Cruncher knuckled his forehead, as Sydney Carton and the spy returned from the dark room. "Adieu, Mr. Barsad," said the former; "our arrangement thus made, you have nothing to fear from me."

He sat down in a chair on the hearth, over

against Mr. Lorry. When they were alone, Mr. Lorry asked him what he had done?

"Not much. If it should go ill with the prisoner, I have ensured access to him, once."

Mr. Lorry's countenance fell.

"It is all I could do," said Carton. "To propose too much, would be to put this man's head under the axe, and, as he himself said, nothing worse could happen to him if he were denounced. It was obviously the weakness of the position. There is no help for it."

"But access to him," said Mr. Lorry, "if it should go ill before the Tribunal, will not save him."

"I never said it would."

Mr. Lorry's eyes gradually sought the fire; his sympathy with his darling, and the heavy disappointment of his second arrest, gradually weakened them; he was an old man now, overborne with anxiety of late, and his tears fell.

"You are a good man and a true friend," said Carton, in an altered voice. "Forgive me if I notice that you are affected. I could not see my father weep, and sit by, careless. And I could not respect your sorrow more, if you were my father. You are free from that misfortune, however."

Though he said the last words, with a slip into his usual manner, there was a true feeling and respect both in his tone and in his touch, that Mr. Lorry, who had never seen the better side of him, was wholly unprepared for. He gave him his hand, and Carton gently pressed it.

"To return to poor Darnay," said Carton. "Don't tell Her of this interview, or this arrangement. It would not enable Her to go to see him. She might think it was contrived, in case of the worse, to convey to him the means of anticipating the sentence."

Mr. Lorry had not thought of that, and he looked quickly at Carton to see if it were in his mind. It seemed to be; he returned the look, and evidently understood it.

"She might think a thousand things,"

Carton said, “and any of them would only add to her trouble. Don’t speak of me to her. As I said to you when I first came, I had better not see her. I can put my hand out, to do any little helpful work for her that my hand can find to do, without that. You are going to her, I hope? She must be very desolate to-night.”

“I am going now, directly.”

“I am glad of that. She has such a strong attachment to you and reliance on you. How does she look?”

“Anxious and unhappy, but very beautiful.”

“Ah!”

It was a long, grieving sound, like a sigh – almost like a sob. It attracted Mr. Lorry’s eyes to Carton’s face, which was turned to the fire. A light, or a shade (the old gentleman could not have said which), passed from it as swiftly as a change will sweep over a hill-side on a wild bright day, and he lifted his foot to put back one of the little flaming logs, which was tumbling forward. He wore the white riding-coat and top-boots, then in vogue, and the light of the fire touching their light surfaces made him look very pale, with his long brown hair, all untrimmed, hanging loose about him. His indifference to fire was sufficiently remarkable to elicit a word of remonstrance from Mr. Lorry; his boot was still upon the hot embers of the flaming log, when it had broken under the weight of his foot.

"I forgot it," he said.

Mr. Lorry's eyes were again attracted to his face. Taking note of the wasted air which clouded the naturally handsome features, and having the expression of prisoners' faces fresh in his mind, he was strongly reminded of that expression.

"And your duties here have drawn to an end, sir?" said Carton, turning to him.

"Yes. As I was telling you last night when Lucie came in so unexpectedly, I have at length done all that I can do here. I hoped to have left them in perfect safety, and then to have quitted Paris. I have my Leave to

Pass. I was ready to go."

They were both silent.

"Yours is a long life to look back upon, sir?" said Carton, wistfully.

"I am in my seventy-eighth year."

"You have been useful all your life; steadily and constantly occupied; trusted, respected, and looked up to?"

"I have been a man of business, ever since I have been a man. Indeed, I may say that I was a man of business when a boy."

"See what a place you fill at seventy-eight. How many people will miss you when you leave it empty!"

"A solitary old bachelor," answered Mr. Lorry, shaking his head. "There is nobody to weep for me."

"How can you say that? Wouldn't She weep for you? Wouldn't her child?"

"Yes, yes, thank God. I didn't quite mean what I said."

"It **is** a thing to thank God for; is it not?"

"Surely, surely."

"If you could say, with truth, to your own solitary heart, to-night, 'I have secured to myself the love and attachment, the gratitude or respect, of no human creature; I have won myself a tender place in no regard; I have done nothing good or serviceable to be remembered by!' your seventy-eight years would be seventy-eight heavy curses; would they not?"

"You say truly, Mr. Carton; I think they would be."

Sydney turned his eyes again upon the fire, and, after a silence of a few moments, said:

"I should like to ask you: – Does your childhood seem far off? Do the days when you sat at your mother's knee, seem days of very long ago?"

Responding to his softened manner, Mr. Lorry answered:

"Twenty years back, yes; at this time of my life, no. For, as I draw closer and closer to the end, I travel in the circle, nearer and nearer to the beginning. It seems to be one of the kind smoothings and preparings of the way. My heart is touched now, by many remembrances that had long fallen asleep, of my pretty young mother (and I so old!), and by many associations of the days when what we call the World was not so real with me, and my faults were not confirmed in me."

"I understand the feeling!" exclaimed Carton, with a bright flush. "And you are the better for it?"

"I hope so."

Carton terminated the conversation here, by rising to help him on with his outer coat; "But you," said Mr. Lorry, reverting to the theme, "you are young."

"Yes," said Carton. "I am not old, but my young way was never the way to age. Enough of me."

"And of me, I am sure," said Mr. Lorry. "Are you going out?"

"I'll walk with you to her gate. You know

my vagabond and restless habits. If I should prowl about the streets a long time, don't be uneasy; I shall reappear in the morning. You go to the Court to-morrow?"

"Yes, unhappily."

"I shall be there, but only as one of the crowd. My Spy will find a place for me. Take my arm, sir."

Mr. Lorry did so, and they went down-stairs and out in the streets. A few minutes brought them to Mr. Lorry's destination. Carton left him there; but lingered at a little distance, and turned back to the gate again when it was shut, and touched it. He had heard of her going to the prison every day. "She came out here," he said, looking about him, "turned this way, must have trod on these stones often. Let me follow in her steps."

It was ten o'clock at night when he stood before the prison of La Force, where she had stood hundreds of times. A little wood-sawyer, having closed his shop, was smoking his pipe at his shop-door.

"Good night, citizen," said Sydney Carton, pausing in going by; for, the man eyed him inquisitively.

"Good night, citizen."

"How goes the Republic?"

"You mean the Guillotine. Not ill. Sixty-three to-day. We shall mount to a hundred soon. Samson and his men complain sometimes, of being exhausted. Ha, ha, ha! He is so droll, that Samson. Such a Barber!"

"Do you often go to see him – "

"Shave? Always. Every day. What a barber! You have seen him at work?"

"Never."

"Go and see him when he has a good batch. Figure this to yourself, citizen; he shaved the sixty-three to-day, in less than two pipes! Less than two pipes. Word of honour!"

As the grinning little man held out the pipe he was smoking, to explain how he timed the executioner, Carton was so sensible of a rising desire to strike the life out of him, that he turned away.

"But you are not English," said the wood-sawyer, "though you wear English dress?"

"Yes," said Carton, pausing again, and answering over his shoulder.

"You speak like a Frenchman."

"I am an old student here."

"Aha, a perfect Frenchman! Good night, Englishman."

"Good night, citizen."

"But go and see that droll dog," the little man persisted, calling after him. "And take a pipe with you!"

Sydney had not gone far out of sight, when he stopped in the middle of the street under a glimmering lamp, and wrote with his pencil on a scrap of paper. Then, traversing with the decided step of one who remembered the way well, several dark and dirty streets – much dirtier than usual, for the best public thoroughfares remained uncleansed in those times of terror – he stopped at a chemist's shop, which the owner was closing with his own hands. A small, dim, crooked shop, kept in a tortuous, up-hill thoroughfare, by a small, dim, crooked man.

Giving this citizen, too, good night, as he confronted him at his counter, he laid the scrap of paper before him. “Whew!” the chemist whistled softly, as he read it. “Hi! hi! hi!”

Sydney Carton took no heed, and the chemist said:

“For you, citizen?”

“For me.”

“You will be careful to keep them separate, citizen? You know the consequences of mixing them?”

“Perfectly.”

Certain small packets were made and given to him. He put them, one by one, in the breast of his inner coat, counted out the money for them, and deliberately left the shop. “There is nothing more to do,” said he, glancing upward at the moon, “until to-morrow. I can’t sleep.”

It was not a reckless manner, the manner in which he said these words aloud under the fast-sailing clouds, nor was it more expressive of negligence than defiance. It was the settled manner of a tired man, who had wandered and struggled and got lost, but who at length struck into his road and saw its end.

Long ago, when he had been famous among his earliest competitors as a youth of great promise, he had followed his father to the grave. His mother had died, years before. These solemn words, which had been read at his father's grave, arose in his mind as he went down the dark streets, among the heavy shadows, with the moon and the clouds sailing on high above him. "I am the resurrection and the life, saith the Lord: he that believeth in me, though he were dead, yet shall he live: and whosoever liveth and believeth in me, shall never die."

In a city dominated by the axe, alone at night, with natural sorrow rising in him for the sixty-three who had been that day put to death, and for to-morrow's victims then awaiting their doom in the prisons, and still of to-morrow's and to-morrow's, the chain of association that brought the words home, like a rusty old ship's anchor from the deep, might have been easily found. He did not seek it, but repeated them and went on.

With a solemn interest in the lighted windows where the people were going to rest, forgetful through a few calm hours of the horrors surrounding them; in the towers of the churches, where no prayers were said, for the popular revulsion had even travelled that length of self-destruction from years of priestly impostors, plunderers, and profligates; in the distant burial-places, reserved, as they wrote upon the gates, for Eternal Sleep; in the abounding gaols; and in the streets along which the sixties rolled to a death which had become so common and material, that no sorrowful story of a haunting Spirit ever arose among the people out of all the working of the Guillotine; with a solemn interest in the whole life and death of the city settling down to its short nightly pause in fury; Sydney Carton crossed the Seine again for the lighter streets.

Few coaches were abroad, for riders in coaches were liable to be suspected, and gentility hid its head in red nightcaps, and put on heavy shoes, and trudged. But, the theatres were all well filled, and the people poured cheerfully out as he passed, and went chatting home. At one of the theatre doors, there was a little girl with a mother, looking for a way across the street through the mud. He carried the child over, and before the timid arm was loosed from his neck asked her for a kiss.

"I am the resurrection and the life, saith the Lord: he that believeth in me, though he were dead, yet shall he live: and whosoever liveth and believeth in me, shall never die."

Now, that the streets were quiet, and the night wore on, the words were in the echoes of his feet, and were in the air. Perfectly calm and steady, he sometimes repeated them to himself as he walked; but, he heard them always.

The night wore out, and, as he stood upon the bridge listening to the water as it splashed the river-walls of the Island of Paris, where the picturesque confusion of houses and cathedral shone bright in the light of the moon, the day came coldly, looking like a dead face out of the sky. Then, the night, with the moon and the stars, turned pale and died, and for a little while it seemed as if Creation were delivered over to Death's dominion.

But, the glorious sun, rising, seemed to strike those words, that burden of the night, straight and warm to his heart in its long bright rays. And looking along them, with reverently shaded eyes, a bridge of light appeared to span the air between him and the sun, while the river sparkled under it.

The strong tide, so swift, so deep, and

certain, was like a congenial friend, in the morning stillness. He walked by the stream, far from the houses, and in the light and warmth of the sun fell asleep on the bank. When he awoke and was afoot again, he lingered there yet a little longer, watching an eddy that turned and turned purposeless, until the stream absorbed it, and carried it on to the sea. – "Like me."

A trading-boat, with a sail of the softened colour of a dead leaf, then glided into his view, floated by him, and died away. As its silent track in the water disappeared, the prayer that had broken up out of his heart for a merciful consideration of all his poor blindnesses and errors, ended in the words, "I am the resurrection and the life."

Mr. Lorry was already out when he got back, and it was easy to surmise where the good old man was gone. Sydney Carton drank nothing but a little coffee, ate some bread, and, having washed and changed to refresh himself, went out to the place of trial.

The court was all astir and a-buzz, when the black sheep – whom many fell away from in dread – pressed him into an obscure corner among the crowd. Mr. Lorry was there, and Doctor Manette was there. She was there, sitting beside her father.

When her husband was brought in, she turned a look upon him, so sustaining, so encouraging, so full of admiring love and pitying tenderness, yet so courageous for his sake, that it called the healthy blood into his face, brightened his glance, and animated his heart. If there had been any eyes to notice the influence of her look, on Sydney Carton, it would have been seen to be the same influence exactly.

Before that unjust Tribunal, there was little or no order of procedure, ensuring to any accused person any reasonable hearing. There could have been no such Revolution, if all laws, forms, and ceremonies, had not first been so monstrously abused, that the suicidal vengeance of the Revolution was to scatter them all to the winds.

Every eye was turned to the jury. The same determined patriots and good republicans as yesterday and the day before, and to-morrow and the day after. Eager and prominent among them, one man with a craving face, and his fingers perpetually hovering about his lips, whose appearance gave great satisfaction to the spectators. A life-thirsting, cannibal-looking, bloody-minded juryman, the Jacques Three of St. Antoine. The whole jury, as a jury of dogs empannelled to try the deer.

Every eye then turned to the five judges and the public prosecutor. No favourable leaning in that quarter to-day. A fell, uncompromising, murderous business-meaning there. Every eye then sought some other eye in the crowd, and gleamed at it approvingly; and heads nodded at one another, before bending forward with a strained attention.

Charles Evremonde, called Darnay. Released yesterday. Reaccused and retaken yesterday. Indictment delivered to him last night. Suspected and Denounced enemy of the Republic, Aristocrat, one of a family of tyrants, one of a race proscribed, for that they had used their abolished privileges to the infamous oppression of the people. Charles Evremonde, called Darnay, in right of such proscription, absolutely Dead in Law.

To this effect, in as few or fewer words, the Public Prosecutor.

The President asked, was the Accused openly denounced or secretly?

"Openly, President."

"By whom?"

"Three voices. Ernest Defarge, wine-vendor of St. Antoine."

"Good."

"Therese Defarge, his wife."

"Good."

"Alexandre Manette, physician."

A great uproar took place in the court, and in the midst of it, Doctor Manette was seen, pale and trembling, standing where he had been seated.

“President, I indignantly protest to you that this is a forgery and a fraud. You know the accused to be the husband of my daughter. My daughter, and those dear to her, are far dearer to me than my life. Who and where is the false conspirator who says that I denounce the husband of my child!”

“Citizen Manette, be tranquil. To fail in submission to the authority of the Tribunal would be to put yourself out of Law. As to what is dearer to you than life, nothing can be so dear to a good citizen as the Republic.”

Loud acclamations hailed this rebuke. The President rang his bell, and with warmth resumed.

“If the Republic should demand of you the sacrifice of your child herself, you would have no duty but to sacrifice her. Listen to what is to follow. In the meanwhile, be silent!"

Frantic acclamations were again raised. Doctor Manette sat down, with his eyes looking around, and his lips trembling; his daughter drew closer to him. The craving man on the jury rubbed his hands together, and restored the usual hand to his mouth.

Defarge was produced, when the court was quiet enough to admit of his being heard, and rapidly expounded the story of the imprisonment, and of his having been a mere boy in the Doctor's service, and of the release, and of the state of the prisoner when released and delivered to him. This short examination followed, for the court was quick with its work.

"You did good service at the taking of the Bastille, citizen?"

"I believe so."

Here, an excited woman screeched from the crowd: "You were one of the best patriots there. Why not say so? You were a cannonier that day there, and you were among the first to enter the accursed fortress when it fell. Patriots, I speak the truth!"

It was The Vengeance who, amidst the warm commendations of the audience, thus assisted the proceedings. The President rang his bell; but, The Vengeance, warming with encouragement, shrieked, "I defy that bell!" wherein she was likewise much commended.

"Inform the Tribunal of what you did that day within the Bastille, citizen."

"I knew," said Defarge, looking down at his wife, who stood at the bottom of the steps on which he was raised, looking steadily up at him; "I knew that this prisoner, of whom I speak, had been confined in a cell known as One Hundred and Five, North Tower. I knew it from himself. He knew himself by no other name than One Hundred and Five, North Tower, when he made shoes under my care. As I serve my gun that day, I resolve, when the place shall fall, to examine that cell. It falls. I mount to the cell, with a fellow-citizen who is one of the Jury, directed by a gaoler. I examine it, very closely. In a hole in the chimney, where a stone has been worked out and replaced, I find a written paper. This is that written paper. I have made it my business to examine some specimens of the writing of Doctor Manette. This is the writing of Doctor Manette. I confide this paper, in the writing of Doctor Manette, to the hands of the President."

"Let it be read."

In a dead silence and stillness – the prisoner under trial looking lovingly at his wife, his wife only looking from him to look with solicitude at her father, Doctor Manette keeping his eyes fixed on the reader, Madame Defarge never taking hers from the prisoner, Defarge never taking his from his feasting wife, and all the other eyes there intent upon the Doctor, who saw none of them – the paper was read, as follows.

CHAPTER TEN

The Substance of the Shadow

I, ALEXANDRE MANETTE, unfortunate physician, native of Beauvais, and afterwards resident in Paris, write this melancholy paper in my doleful cell in the Bastille, during the last month of the year, 1767. I write it at stolen intervals, under every difficulty. I design to secrete it in the wall of the chimney, where I have slowly and laboriously made a place of concealment for it. Some pitying hand may find it there, when I and my sorrows are dust.

"These words are formed by the rusty iron point with which I write with difficulty in scrapings of soot and charcoal from the chimney, mixed with blood, in the last month of the tenth year of my captivity. Hope has quite departed from my breast. I know from terrible warnings I have noted in myself that my reason will not long remain unimpaired, but I solemnly declare that I am at this time in the possession of my right mind – that my memory is exact and circumstantial – and that I write the truth as I shall answer for these my last recorded words, whether they be ever read by men or not, at the Eternal Judgment-seat.

"One cloudy moonlight night, in the third week of December (I think the twenty-second of the month) in the year 1757, I was walking on a retired part of the quay by the Seine for the refreshment of the frosty air, at an hour's distance from my place of residence in the Street of the School of Medicine, when a carriage came along behind me, driven very fast. As I stood aside to let that carriage pass, apprehensive that it might otherwise run me down, a head was put out at the window, and a voice called to the driver to stop.

"The carriage stopped as soon as the driver could rein in his horses, and the same voice called to me by my name. I answered. The carriage was then so far in advance of me that two gentlemen had time to open the door and alight before I came up with it.

"I observed that they were both wrapped in cloaks, and appeared to conceal themselves. As they stood side by side near the carriage door, I also observed that they both looked of about my own age, or rather younger, and that they were greatly alike, in stature, manner, voice, and (as far as I could see) face too.

"'You are Doctor Manette?' said one.

"I am."

"'Doctor Manette, formerly of Beauvais,' said the other; 'the young physician, originally an expert surgeon, who within the last year or two has made a rising reputation in Paris?'

"'Gentlemen,' I returned, 'I am that Doctor Manette of whom you speak so graciously.'

"'We have been to your residence,' said the first, 'and not being so fortunate as to find you there, and being informed that you were probably walking in this direction, we followed, in the hope of overtaking you. Will you please to enter the carriage?'

"The manner of both was imperious, and they both moved, as these words were spoken, so as to place me between themselves and the carriage door. They were armed. I was not.

"'Gentlemen,' said I, 'pardon me; but I usually inquire who does me the honour to seek my assistance, and what is the nature of the case to which I am summoned.'

"The reply to this was made by him who

had spoken second. 'Doctor, your clients are people of condition. As to the nature of the case, our confidence in your skill assures us that you will ascertain it for yourself better than we can describe it. Enough. Will you please to enter the carriage?'

"I could do nothing but comply, and I entered it in silence. They both entered after me – the last springing in, after putting up the steps. The carriage turned about, and drove on at its former speed.

"I repeat this conversation exactly as it occurred. I have no doubt that it is, word for word, the same. I describe everything exactly as it took place, constraining my mind not to wander from the task. Where I make the broken marks that follow here, I leave off for the time, and put my paper in its hiding-place.

"The carriage left the streets behind, passed the North Barrier, and emerged upon the country road. At two-thirds of a league from the Barrier – I did not estimate the distance at that time, but afterwards when I traversed it – it struck out of the main avenue, and presently stopped at a solitary house, We all three alighted, and walked, by a damp soft footpath in a garden where a neglected fountain had overflowed, to the door of the house. It was not opened immediately, in answer to the ringing of the bell, and one of my two conductors struck the man who opened it, with his heavy riding glove, across the face.

"There was nothing in this action to attract my particular attention, for I had seen common people struck more commonly than dogs. But, the other of the two, being angry likewise, struck the man in like manner with his arm; the look and bearing of the brothers were then so exactly alike, that I then first perceived them to be twin brothers.

"From the time of our alighting at the outer gate (which we found locked, and which one of the brothers had opened to admit us, and had relocked), I had heard cries proceeding from an upper chamber. I was conducted to this chamber straight, the cries growing louder as we ascended the stairs, and I found a patient in a high fever of the brain, lying on a bed.

"The patient was a woman of great beauty, and young; assuredly not much past twenty. Her hair was torn and ragged, and her arms were bound to her sides with sashes and handkerchiefs. I noticed that these bonds were all portions of a gentleman's dress. On one of them, which was a fringed scarf for a dress of ceremony, I saw the armorial bearings of a Noble, and the letter E.

"I saw this, within the first minute of my contemplation of the patient; for, in her restless strivings she had turned over on her face on the edge of the bed, had drawn the end of the scarf into her mouth, and was in danger of suffocation. My first act was to put out my hand to relieve her breathing; and in moving the scarf aside, the embroidery in the corner caught my sight.

"I turned her gently over, placed my hands upon her breast to calm her and keep her down, and looked into her face. Her eyes were dilated and wild, and she constantly uttered piercing shrieks, and repeated the words, 'My husband, my father, and my brother!' and then counted up to twelve, and said, 'Hush!' For an instant, and no more, she would pause to listen, and then the piercing shrieks would begin again, and she would repeat the cry, 'My husband, my father, and my brother!' and would count up to twelve, and say, 'Hush!' There was no variation in the order, or the manner. There was no cessation, but the regular moment's pause, in the utterance of these sounds.

"'How long,' I asked, 'has this lasted?'

"To distinguish the brothers, I will call them the elder and the younger; by the elder, I mean him who exercised the most authority. It was the elder who replied, 'Since about this hour last night.'

"'She has a husband, a father, and a brother?'

"'A brother.'

"'I do not address her brother?'

"He answered with great contempt, 'No.'

"'She has some recent association with the number twelve?'

"The younger brother impatiently rejoined, 'With twelve o'clock?'

"'See, gentlemen,' said I, still keeping my hands upon her breast, 'how useless I am, as you have brought me! If I had known what I was coming to see, I could have come provided. As it is, time must be lost. There are no medicines to be obtained in this lonely place.'

"The elder brother looked to the younger, who said haughtily, 'There is a case of medicines here;' and brought it from a closet, and put it on the table.

"I opened some of the bottles, smelt them, and put the stoppers to my lips. If I had wanted to use anything save narcotic medicines that were poisons in themselves, I would not have administered any of those.

"'Do you doubt them?' asked the younger brother.

"'You see, monsieur, I am going to use them,' I replied, and said no more.

"I made the patient swallow, with great difficulty, and after many efforts, the dose that I desired to give. As I intended to repeat it after a while, and as it was necessary to watch its influence, I then sat down by the side of the bed. There was a timid and suppressed woman in attendance (wife of the man down-stairs), who had retreated into a corner. The house was damp and decayed, indifferently furnished – evidently, recently occupied and temporarily used. Some thick old hangings had been nailed up before the windows, to deaden the sound of the shrieks. They continued to be uttered in their regular succession, with the cry, 'My husband, my father, and my brother!' the counting up to twelve, and 'Hush!' The frenzy was so violent, that I had not unfastened the bandages restraining the arms; but, I had looked to them, to see that they were not painful. The only spark of encouragement in the case, was, that my hand upon the sufferer's breast had this much soothing influence, that for minutes at a time it tranquillised the figure. It had no effect upon the cries; no pendulum could be more regular.

"For the reason that my hand had this effect (I assume), I had sat by the side of the bed for half an hour, with the two brothers looking on, before the elder said:

"'There is another patient.'

"I was startled, and asked, 'Is it a pressing case?'

"'You had better see,' he carelessly answered; and took up a light.

"The other patient lay in a back room across a second staircase, which was a species of loft over a stable. There was a low plastered ceiling to a part of it; the rest was open, to the ridge of the tiled roof, and there were beams across. Hay and straw were stored in that portion of the place, fagots for firing, and a heap of apples in sand. I had to pass through that part, to get at the other. My memory is circumstantial and unshaken. I try it with these details, and I see them all, in this my cell in the Bastille, near the close of the tenth year of my captivity, as I saw them all that night.

"On some hay on the ground, with a cushion thrown under his head, lay a handsome peasant boy – a boy of not more than seventeen at the most. He lay on his back, with his teeth set, his right hand clenched on his breast, and his glaring eyes looking straight upward. I could not see where his wound was, as I kneeled on one knee over him; but, I could see that he was dying of a wound from a sharp point.

"'I am a doctor, my poor fellow,' said I. 'Let

me examine it.'

"'I do not want it examined,' he answered; 'let it be.'

"It was under his hand, and I soothed him to let me move his hand away. The wound was a sword-thrust, received from twenty to twenty-four hours before, but no skill could have saved him if it had been looked to without delay. He was then dying fast. As I turned my eyes to the elder brother, I saw him looking down at this handsome boy whose life was ebbing out, as if he were a wounded bird, or hare, or rabbit; not at all as if he were a fellow-creature.

"'How has this been done, monsieur?' said I.

"'A crazed young common dog! A serf! Forced my brother to draw upon him, and has fallen by my brother's sword – like a gentleman.'

"There was no touch of pity, sorrow, or kindred humanity, in this answer. The speaker seemed to acknowledge that it was inconvenient to have that different order of creature dying there, and that it would have been better if he had died in the usual obscure routine of his vermin kind. He was quite incapable of any compassionate feeling about the boy, or about his fate.

"The boy's eyes had slowly moved to him as he had spoken, and they now slowly moved to me.

"'Doctor, they are very proud, these Nobles; but we common dogs are proud too, sometimes. They plunder us, outrage us, beat us, kill us; but we have a little pride left, sometimes. She – have you seen her, Doctor?'

"The shrieks and the cries were audible there, though subdued by the distance. He referred to them, as if she were lying in our presence.

"I said, 'I have seen her.'

"'She is my sister, Doctor. They have had their shameful rights, these Nobles, in the modesty and virtue of our sisters, many years, but we have had good girls among us. I know it, and have heard my father say so. She was a good girl. She was betrothed to a good young man, too: a tenant of his. We were all tenants of his – that man's who stands there. The other is his brother, the worst of a bad race.'

"It was with the greatest difficulty that the boy gathered bodily force to speak; but, his spirit spoke with a dreadful emphasis.

"'We were so robbed by that man who stands there, as all we common dogs are by those superior Beings – taxed by him without mercy, obliged to work for him without pay, obliged to grind our corn at his mill, obliged to feed scores of his tame birds on our wretched crops, and forbidden for our lives to keep a single tame bird of our own, pillaged and plundered to that degree that when we chanced to have a bit of meat, we ate it in fear, with the door barred and the shutters closed, that his people should not see it and take it from us – I say, we were so robbed, and hunted, and were made so poor, that our father told us it was a dreadful thing to bring a child into the world, and that what we should most pray for, was, that our women might be barren and our miserable race die out!'

"I had never before seen the sense of being oppressed, bursting forth like a fire. I had supposed that it must be latent in the people somewhere; but, I had never seen it break out, until I saw it in the dying boy.

"'Nevertheless, Doctor, my sister married. He was ailing at that time, poor fellow, and she married her lover, that she might tend and comfort him in our cottage – our dog-hut, as that man would call it. She had not been married many weeks, when that man's brother saw her and admired her, and asked that man to lend her to him – for what are husbands among us! He was willing enough, but my sister was good and virtuous, and hated his brother with a hatred as strong as mine. What did the two then, to persuade her husband to use his influence with her, to make her willing?'

"The boy's eyes, which had been fixed on mine, slowly turned to the looker-on, and I saw in the two faces that all he said was true. The two opposing kinds of pride confronting one another, I can see, even in this Bastille; the gentleman's, all negligent indifference; the peasant's, all trodden-down sentiment, and passionate revenge.

"'You know, Doctor, that it is among the Rights of these Nobles to harness us common dogs to carts, and drive us. They so harnessed him and drove him. You know that it is among their Rights to keep us in their grounds all night, quieting the frogs, in order that their noble sleep may not be disturbed. They kept him out in the unwholesome mists at night, and ordered him back into his harness in the day. But he was not persuaded. No! Taken out of harness one day at noon, to feed – if he could find food – he sobbed twelve times, once for every stroke of the bell, and died on her bosom.'

"Nothing human could have held life in the boy but his determination to tell all his wrong. He forced back the gathering shadows of death, as he forced his clenched right hand to remain clenched, and to cover his wound.

"'Then, with that man's permission and even with his aid, his brother took her away; in spite of what I know she must have told his brother – and what that is, will not be long unknown to you, Doctor, if it is now – his brother took her away – for his pleasure and diversion, for a little while. I saw her pass me on the road. When I took the tidings home, our father's heart burst; he never spoke one of the words that filled it. I took my young sister (for I have another) to a place beyond the reach of this man, and where, at least, she will never be **his** vassal. Then, I tracked the brother here, and last night climbed in – a common dog, but sword in hand. – Where is the loft window?

It was somewhere here?'

"The room was darkening to his sight; the world was narrowing around him. I glanced about me, and saw that the hay and straw were trampled over the floor, as if there had been a struggle.

"'She heard me, and ran in. I told her not to come near us till he was dead. He came in and first tossed me some pieces of money; then struck at me with a whip. But I, though a common dog, so struck at him as to make him draw. Let him break into as many pieces as he will, the sword that he stained with my common blood; he drew to defend himself – thrust at me with all his skill for his life.'

"My glance had fallen, but a few moments before, on the fragments of a broken sword, lying among the hay. That weapon was a gentleman's. In another place, lay an old sword that seemed to have been a soldier's.

"'Now, lift me up, Doctor; lift me up. Where is he?'

"'He is not here,' I said, supporting the boy, and thinking that he referred to the brother.

"'He! Proud as these nobles are, he is afraid to see me. Where is the man who was here? Turn my face to him.'

"I did so, raising the boy's head against my knee. But, invested for the moment with extraordinary power, he raised himself completely: obliging me to rise too, or I could not have still supported him.

"'Marquis,' said the boy, turned to him with his eyes opened wide, and his right hand raised, 'in the days when all these things are to be answered for, I summon you and yours, to the last of your bad race, to answer for them. I mark this cross of blood upon you, as a sign that I do it. In the days when all these things are to be answered for, I summon your brother, the worst of the bad race, to answer for them separately. I mark this cross of blood upon him, as a sign that I do it.'

"Twice, he put his hand to the wound in

his breast, and with his forefinger drew a cross in the air. He stood for an instant with the finger yet raised, and as it dropped, he dropped with it, and I laid him down dead.

"When I returned to the bedside of the young woman, I found her raving in precisely the same order of continuity. I knew that this might last for many hours, and that it would probably end in the silence of the grave.

"I repeated the medicines I had given her, and I sat at the side of the bed until the night was far advanced. She never abated the piercing quality of her shrieks, never stumbled in the distinctness or the order of her words. They were always 'My husband, my father, and my brother! One, two, three, four, five, six, seven, eight, nine, ten, eleven, twelve. Hush!'

"This lasted twenty-six hours from the time when I first saw her. I had come and gone twice, and was again sitting by her, when she began to falter. I did what little could be done to assist that opportunity, and by-and-bye she sank into a lethargy, and lay like the dead.

"It was as if the wind and rain had lulled at last, after a long and fearful storm. I released her arms, and called the woman to assist me to compose her figure and the dress she had torn. It was then that I knew her condition to be that of one in whom the first expectations of being a mother have arisen; and it was then that I lost the little hope I had had of her.

"'Is she dead?' asked the Marquis, whom I will still describe as the elder brother, coming booted into the room from his horse.

"'Not dead,' said I; 'but like to die.'

"'What strength there is in these common bodies!' he said, looking down at her with some curiosity.

"'There is prodigious strength,' I answered him, 'in sorrow and despair.'

"He first laughed at my words, and then frowned at them. He moved a chair with his foot near to mine, ordered the woman away, and said in a subdued voice,

"'Doctor, finding my brother in this difficulty with these hinds, I recommended that your aid should be invited. Your reputation is high, and, as a young man with your fortune to make, you are probably mindful of your interest. The things that you see here, are things to be seen, and not spoken of.'

"I listened to the patient's breathing, and avoided answering.

"'Do you honour me with your attention, Doctor?'

"'Monsieur,' said I, 'in my profession, the communications of patients are always received in confidence.' I was guarded in my answer, for I was troubled in my mind with what I had heard and seen.

"Her breathing was so difficult to trace, that I carefully tried the pulse and the heart. There was life, and no more. Looking round as I resumed my seat, I found both the brothers intent upon me.

"I write with so much difficulty, the cold is so severe, I am so fearful of being detected and consigned to an underground cell and total darkness, that I must abridge this narrative. There is no confusion or failure in my memory; it can recall, and could detail, every word that was ever spoken between me and those brothers.

"She lingered for a week. Towards the last, I could understand some few syllables that she said to me, by placing my ear close to her lips. She asked me where she was, and I told her; who I was, and I told her. It was in vain that I asked her for her family name. She faintly shook her head upon the pillow, and kept her secret, as the boy had done.

"I had no opportunity of asking her any question, until I had told the brothers she was sinking fast, and could not live another day. Until then, though no one was ever presented to her consciousness save the woman and myself, one or other of them had always jealously sat behind the curtain at the head of the bed when I was there. But when it came to that, they seemed careless what communication I might hold with her; as if – the thought passed through my mind – I were dying too.

"I always observed that their pride bitterly resented the younger brother's (as I call him) having crossed swords with a peasant, and that peasant a boy. The only consideration that appeared to affect the mind of either of them was the consideration that this was highly degrading to the family, and was ridiculous. As often as I caught the younger brother's eyes, their expression reminded me that he disliked me deeply, for knowing what I knew from the boy. He was smoother and more polite to me than the elder; but I saw this. I also saw that I was an incumbrance in the mind of the elder, too.

"My patient died, two hours before midnight – at a time, by my watch, answering almost to the minute when I had first seen her. I was alone with her, when her forlorn young head drooped gently on one side, and all her earthly wrongs and sorrows ended.

“The brothers were waiting in a room downstairs, impatient to ride away. I had heard them, alone at the bedside, striking their boots with their riding-whips, and loitering up and down.

“‘At last she is dead?’ said the elder, when I went in.

“‘She is dead,’ said I.

“‘I congratulate you, my brother,’ were his words as he turned round.

“He had before offered me money, which I had postponed taking. He now gave me a rouleau of gold. I took it from his hand, but laid it on the table. I had considered the question, and had resolved to accept nothing.

“‘Pray excuse me,’ said I. ‘Under the circumstances, no.’

“They exchanged looks, but bent their heads to me as I bent mine to them, and we parted without another word on either side.

"I am weary, weary, weary – worn down by misery. I cannot read what I have written with this gaunt hand.

"Early in the morning, the rouleau of gold was left at my door in a little box, with my name on the outside. From the first, I had anxiously considered what I ought to do. I decided, that day, to write privately to the Minister, stating the nature of the two cases to which I had been summoned, and the place to which I had gone: in effect, stating all the circumstances. I knew what Court influence was, and what the immunities of the Nobles were, and I expected that the matter would never be heard of; but, I wished to relieve my own mind. I had kept the matter a profound secret, even from my wife; and this, too, I resolved to state in my letter. I had no apprehension whatever of my real danger; but I was conscious that there might be danger for others, if others were compromised by possessing the knowledge that I possessed.

"I was much engaged that day, and could not complete my letter that night. I rose long before my usual time next morning to finish it. It was the last day of the year. The letter was lying before me just completed, when I was told that a lady waited, who wished to see me.

"I am growing more and more unequal to the task I have set myself. It is so cold, so dark, my senses are so benumbed, and the gloom upon me is so dreadful.

"The lady was young, engaging, and handsome, but not marked for long life. She was in great agitation. She presented herself to me as the wife of the Marquis St. Evremonde. I connected the title by which the boy had addressed the elder brother, with the initial letter embroidered on the scarf, and had no difficulty in arriving at the conclusion that I had seen that nobleman very lately.

"My memory is still accurate, but I cannot write the words of our conversation. I suspect that I am watched more closely than I was, and I know not at what times I may be watched. She had in part suspected, and in part discovered, the main facts of the cruel story, of her husband's share in it, and my being resorted to. She did not know that the girl was dead. Her hope had been, she said in great distress, to show her, in secret, a woman's sympathy. Her hope had been to avert the wrath of Heaven from a House that had long been hateful to the suffering many.

"She had reasons for believing that there was a young sister living, and her greatest desire was, to help that sister. I could tell her nothing but that there was such a sister; beyond that, I knew nothing. Her inducement to come to me, relying on my confidence, had been the hope that I could tell her the name and place of abode. Whereas, to this wretched hour I am ignorant of both.

"These scraps of paper fail me. One was taken from me, with a warning, yesterday. I must finish my record to-day.

"She was a good, compassionate lady, and not happy in her marriage. How could she be! The brother distrusted and disliked her, and his influence was all opposed to her; she stood in dread of him, and in dread of her husband too. When I handed her down to the door, there was a child, a pretty boy from two to three years old, in her carriage.

"'For his sake, Doctor,' she said, pointing to him in tears, 'I would do all I can to make what poor amends I can. He will never prosper in his inheritance otherwise. I have a presentiment that if no other innocent atonement is made for this, it will one day be required of him. What I have left to call my own – it is little beyond the worth of a few jewels – I will make it the first charge of his life to bestow, with the compassion and lamenting of his dead mother, on this injured family, if the sister can be discovered.'

"She kissed the boy, and said, caressing him, 'It is for thine own dear sake. Thou wilt be faithful, little Charles?' The child answered her bravely, 'Yes!' I kissed her hand, and she took him in her arms, and went away caressing him. I never saw her more.

"As she had mentioned her husband's name in the faith that I knew it, I added no mention of it to my letter. I sealed my letter, and, not trusting it out of my own hands, delivered it myself that day.

"That night, the last night of the year, towards nine o'clock, a man in a black dress rang at my gate, demanded to see me, and softly followed my servant, Ernest Defarge, a youth, up-stairs. When my servant came into the room where I sat with my wife – O my wife, beloved of my heart! My fair young English wife! – we saw the man, who was supposed to be at the gate, standing silent behind him.

"An urgent case in the Rue St. Honore, he said. It would not detain me, he had a coach in waiting.

"It brought me here, it brought me to my grave. When I was clear of the house, a black muffler was drawn tightly over my mouth from behind, and my arms were pinioned. The two brothers crossed the road from a dark corner, and identified me with a single gesture. The Marquis took from his pocket the letter I had written, showed it me, burnt it in the light of a lantern that was held, and extinguished the ashes with his foot. Not a word was spoken. I was brought here, I was brought to my living grave.

"If it had pleased **God** to put it in the hard heart of either of the brothers, in all these frightful years, to grant me any tidings of my dearest wife – so much as to let me know by a word whether alive or dead – I might have thought that He had not quite abandoned them. But, now I believe that the mark of the red cross is fatal to them, and that they have no part in His mercies. And them and their descendants, to the last of their race, I, Alexandre Manette, unhappy prisoner, do this last night of the year 1767, in my unbearable agony, denounce to the times when all these things shall be answered for. I denounce them to Heaven and to earth."

A terrible sound arose when the reading of this document was done. A sound of craving and eagerness that had nothing articulate in it but blood. The narrative called up the most revengeful passions of the time, and there was not a head in the nation but must have dropped before it.

Little need, in presence of that tribunal and that auditory, to show how the Defarges had not made the paper public, with the other captured Bastille memorials borne in procession, and had kept it, biding their time. Little need to show that this detested family name had long been anathematised by Saint Antoine, and was wrought into the fatal register. The man never trod ground whose virtues and services would have sustained him in that place that day, against such denunciation.

And all the worse for the doomed man, that the denouncer was a well-known citizen, his own attached friend, the father of his wife. One of the frenzied aspirations of the populace was, for imitations of the questionable public virtues of antiquity, and for sacrifices and self-immolations on the people's altar. Therefore when the President said (else had his own head quivered on his shoulders), that the good physician of the Republic would deserve better still of the Republic by rooting out an obnoxious family of Aristocrats, and would doubtless feel a sacred glow and joy in making his daughter a widow and her child an orphan, there was wild excitement, patriotic fervour, not a touch of human sympathy.

"Much influence around him, has that Doctor?" murmured Madame Defarge, smiling to The Vengeance. "Save him now, my Doctor, save him!"

At every juryman's vote, there was a roar. Another and another. Roar and roar.

Unanimously voted. At heart and by descent an Aristocrat, an enemy of the Republic, a notorious oppressor of the People. Back to the Conciergerie, and Death within four-and-twenty hours!

CHAPTER ELEVEN

Dusk

THE WRETCHED wife of the innocent man thus doomed to die, fell under the sentence, as if she had been mortally stricken. But, she uttered no sound; and so strong was the voice within her, representing that it was she of all the world who must uphold him in his misery and not augment it, that it quickly raised her, even from that shock.

The Judges having to take part in a public demonstration out of doors, the Tribunal adjourned. The quick noise and movement of the court's emptying itself by many passages had not ceased, when Lucie stood stretching out her arms towards her husband, with nothing in her face but love and consolation.

"If I might touch him! If I might embrace him once! O, good citizens, if you would have so much compassion for us!"

There was but a gaoler left, along with two of the four men who had taken him last night, and Barsad. The people had all poured out to the show in the streets. Barsad proposed to the rest, "Let her embrace him then; it is but a moment." It was silently acquiesced in, and they passed her over the seats in the hall to a raised place, where he, by leaning over the dock, could fold her in his arms.

"Farewell, dear darling of my soul. My parting blessing on my love. We shall meet again, where the weary are at rest!"

They were her husband's words, as he held her to his bosom.

"I can bear it, dear Charles. I am supported from above: don't suffer for me. A parting blessing for our child."

"I send it to her by you. I kiss her by you. I say farewell to her by you."

"My husband. No! A moment!" He was tearing himself apart from her. "We shall not be separated long. I feel that this will break my heart by-and-bye; but I will do my duty while I can, and when I leave her, God will raise up friends for her, as He did for me."

Her father had followed her, and would have fallen on his knees to both of them, but that Darnay put out a hand and seized him, crying:

"No, no! What have you done, what have you done, that you should kneel to us! We know now, what a struggle you made of old. We know, now what you underwent when you suspected my descent, and when you knew it. We know now, the natural antipathy you strove against, and conquered, for her dear sake. We thank you with all our hearts, and all our love and duty. Heaven be with you!"

Her father's only answer was to draw his hands through his white hair, and wring them with a shriek of anguish.

"It could not be otherwise," said the prisoner. "All things have worked together as they have fallen out. It was the always-vain endeavour to discharge my poor mother's trust that first brought my fatal presence near you. Good could never come of such evil, a happier end was not in nature to so unhappy a beginning. Be comforted, and forgive me. Heaven bless you!"

As he was drawn away, his wife released him, and stood looking after him with her hands touching one another in the attitude of prayer, and with a radiant look upon her face, in which there was even a comforting smile. As he went out at the prisoners' door, she turned, laid her head lovingly on her father's breast, tried to speak to him, and fell at his feet.

Then, issuing from the obscure corner from which he had never moved, Sydney Carton came and took her up. Only her father and Mr. Lorry were with her. His arm trembled as it raised her, and supported her head. Yet, there was an air about him that was not all of pity – that had a flush of pride in it.

"Shall I take her to a coach? I shall never feel her weight."

He carried her lightly to the door, and laid her tenderly down in a coach. Her father and their old friend got into it, and he took his seat beside the driver.

When they arrived at the gateway where he had paused in the dark not many hours before, to picture to himself on which of the rough stones of the street her feet had trodden, he lifted her again, and carried her up the staircase to their rooms. There, he laid her down on a couch, where her child and Miss Pross wept over her.

"Don't recall her to herself," he said, softly, to the latter, "she is better so. Don't revive her to consciousness, while she only faints."

"Oh, Carton, Carton, dear Carton!" cried little Lucie, springing up and throwing her arms passionately round him, in a burst of grief. "Now that you have come, I think you will do something to help mamma, something to save papa! O, look at her, dear Carton! Can you, of all the people who love her, bear to see her so?"

He bent over the child, and laid her blooming cheek against his face. He put her gently from him, and looked at her unconscious mother.

"Before I go," he said, and paused – "I may kiss her?"

It was remembered afterwards that when he bent down and touched her face with his lips, he murmured some words. The child, who was nearest to him, told them afterwards, and told her grandchildren when she was a handsome old lady, that she heard him say, "A life you love."

When he had gone out into the next room, he turned suddenly on Mr. Lorry and her father, who were following, and said to the latter:

"You had great influence but yesterday, Doctor Manette; let it at least be tried. These judges, and all the men in power, are very friendly to you, and very recognisant of your services; are they not?"

"Nothing connected with Charles was concealed from me. I had the strongest assurances that I should save him; and I did." He returned the answer in great trouble, and very slowly.

"Try them again. The hours between this and to-morrow afternoon are few and short, but try."

"I intend to try. I will not rest a moment."

"That's well. I have known such energy as yours do great things before now – though never," he added, with a smile and a sigh together, "such great things as this. But try!

Of little worth as life is when we misuse it, it is worth that effort. It would cost nothing to lay down if it were not."

"I will go," said Doctor Manette, "to the Prosecutor and the President straight, and I will go to others whom it is better not to name. I will write too, and – But stay! There is a Celebration in the streets, and no one will be accessible until dark."

"That's true. Well! It is a forlorn hope at the best, and not much the forlorner for being delayed till dark. I should like to know how you speed; though, mind! I expect nothing! When are you likely to have seen these dread powers, Doctor Manette?"

"Immediately after dark, I should hope. Within an hour or two from this."

"It will be dark soon after four. Let us stretch the hour or two. If I go to Mr. Lorry's at nine, shall I hear what you have done, either from our friend or from yourself?"

"Yes."

"May you prosper!"

Mr. Lorry followed Sydney to the outer door, and, touching him on the shoulder as he was going away, caused him to turn.

"I have no hope," said Mr. Lorry, in a low and sorrowful whisper.

"Nor have I."

"If any one of these men, or all of these men, were disposed to spare him – which is a large supposition; for what is his life, or any man's to them! – I doubt if they durst spare him after the demonstration in the court."

"And so do I. I heard the fall of the axe in that sound."

Mr. Lorry leaned his arm upon the door-post, and bowed his face upon it.

"Don't despond," said Carton, very gently; "don't grieve. I encouraged Doctor Manette in this idea, because I felt that it might one day be consolatory to her. Otherwise, she might think 'his life was wantonly thrown away or wasted,' and that might trouble her."

"Yes, yes, yes," returned Mr. Lorry, drying

his eyes, "you are right. But he will perish; there is no real hope."

"Yes. He will perish: there is no real hope," echoed Carton.

And walked with a settled step, downstairs.

CHAPTER TWELVE

Darkness

SYDNEY CARTON paused in the street, not quite decided where to go. “At Tellson’s banking-house at nine,” he said, with a musing face. “Shall I do well, in the mean time, to show myself? I think so. It is best that these people should know there is such a man as I here; it is a sound precaution, and may be a necessary preparation. But care, care, care! Let me think it out!”

Checking his steps which had begun to tend towards an object, he took a turn or two in the already darkening street, and traced the thought in his mind to its possible consequences. His first impression was confirmed. "It is best," he said, finally resolved, "that these people should know there is such a man as I here." And he turned his face towards Saint Antoine.

Defarge had described himself, that day, as the keeper of a wine-shop in the Saint Antoine suburb. It was not difficult for one who knew the city well, to find his house without asking any question. Having ascertained its situation, Carton came out of those closer streets again, and dined at a place of refreshment and fell sound asleep after dinner. For the first time in many years, he had no strong drink. Since last night he had taken nothing but a little light thin wine, and last night he had dropped the brandy slowly down on Mr. Lorry's hearth like a man who had done with it.

It was as late as seven o'clock when he awoke refreshed, and went out into the streets again. As he passed along towards Saint Antoine, he stopped at a shop-window where there was a mirror, and slightly altered the disordered arrangement of his loose cravat, and his coat-collar, and his wild hair. This done, he went on direct to Defarge's, and went in.

There happened to be no customer in the shop but Jacques Three, of the restless fingers and the croaking voice. This man, whom he had seen upon the Jury, stood drinking at the little counter, in conversation with the Defarges, man and wife. The Vengeance assisted in the conversation, like a regular member of the establishment.

As Carton walked in, took his seat and asked (in very indifferent French) for a small measure of wine, Madame Defarge cast a careless glance at him, and then a keener, and then a keener, and then advanced to him herself, and asked him what it was he had ordered.

He repeated what he had already said.

"English?" asked Madame Defarge, inquisitively raising her dark eyebrows.

After looking at her, as if the sound of even a single French word were slow to express itself to him, he answered, in his former strong foreign accent. "Yes, madame, yes. I am English!"

Madame Defarge returned to her counter to get the wine, and, as he took up a Jacobin journal and feigned to pore over it puzzling out its meaning, he heard her say, "I swear to you, like Evremonde!"

Defarge brought him the wine, and gave him Good Evening.

"How?"

"Good evening."

"Oh! Good evening, citizen," filling his glass. "Ah! and good wine. I drink to the Republic."

Defarge went back to the counter, and said, "Certainly, a little like." Madame sternly retorted, "I tell you a good deal like." Jacques Three pacifically remarked, "He is so much in your mind, see you, madame." The amiable Vengeance added, with a laugh, "Yes, my faith! And you are looking forward with so much pleasure to seeing him once more to-morrow!"

Carton followed the lines and words of his paper, with a slow forefinger, and with a studious and absorbed face. They were all leaning their arms on the counter close together, speaking low. After a silence of a few moments, during which they all looked towards him without disturbing his outward attention from the Jacobin editor, they resumed their conversation.

"It is true what madame says," observed Jacques Three. "Why stop? There is great force in that. Why stop?"

"Well, well," reasoned Defarge, "but one must stop somewhere. After all, the question is still where?"

"At extermination," said madame.

"Magnificent!" croaked Jacques Three. The Vengeance, also, highly approved.

"Extermination is good doctrine, my wife," said Defarge, rather troubled; "in general, I say nothing against it. But this Doctor has suffered much; you have seen him to-day; you have observed his face when the paper was read."

"I have observed his face!" repeated madame, contemptuously and angrily. "Yes. I have observed his face. I have observed his face to be not the face of a true friend of the Republic. Let him take care of his face!"

"And you have observed, my wife," said Defarge, in a deprecatory manner, "the anguish of his daughter, which must be a dreadful anguish to him!"

"I have observed his daughter," repeated madame; "yes, I have observed his daughter, more times than one. I have observed her to-day, and I have observed her other days. I have observed her in the court, and I have observed her in the street by the prison.

Let me but lift my finger – !" She seemed to raise it (the listener's eyes were always on his paper), and to let it fall with a rattle on the ledge before her, as if the axe had dropped.

"The citizeness is superb!" croaked the Juryman.

"She is an Angel!" said The Vengeance, and embraced her.

"As to thee," pursued madame, implacably, addressing her husband, "if it depended on thee – which, happily, it does not – thou wouldst rescue this man even now."

"No!" protested Defarge. "Not if to lift this glass would do it! But I would leave the matter there. I say, stop there."

"See you then, Jacques," said Madame Defarge, wrathfully; "and see you, too, my little Vengeance; see you both! Listen! For other crimes as tyrants and oppressors, I have this race a long time on my register, doomed to destruction and extermination. Ask my husband, is that so."

"It is so," assented Defarge, without being

asked.

"In the beginning of the great days, when the Bastille falls, he finds this paper of to-day, and he brings it home, and in the middle of the night when this place is clear and shut, we read it, here on this spot, by the light of this lamp. Ask him, is that so."

"It is so," assented Defarge.

"That night, I tell him, when the paper is read through, and the lamp is burnt out, and the day is gleaming in above those shutters and between those iron bars, that I have now a secret to communicate. Ask him, is that so."

"It is so," assented Defarge again.

"I communicate to him that secret. I smite this bosom with these two hands as I smite it now, and I tell him, 'Defarge, I was brought up among the fishermen of the sea-shore, and that peasant family so injured by the two Evremonde brothers, as that Bastille paper describes, is my family. Defarge, that sister of the mortally wounded boy upon the ground was my sister, that husband was my sister's husband, that unborn child was their child, that brother was my brother, that father was my father, those dead are my dead, and that summons to answer for those things descends to me!' Ask him, is that so."

"It is so," assented Defarge once more.

"Then tell Wind and Fire where to stop," returned madame; "but don't tell me."

Both her hearers derived a horrible enjoyment from the deadly nature of her wrath – the listener could feel how white she was, without seeing her – and both highly commended it. Defarge, a weak minority, interposed a few words for the memory of the compassionate wife of the Marquis; but only elicited from his own wife a repetition of her last reply. "Tell the Wind and the Fire where to stop; not me!"

Customers entered, and the group was broken up. The English customer paid for what he had had, perplexedly counted his change, and asked, as a stranger, to be directed towards the National Palace. Madame Defarge took him to the door, and put her arm on his, in pointing out the road. The English customer was not without his reflections then, that it might be a good deed to seize that arm, lift it, and strike under it sharp and deep.

But, he went his way, and was soon swallowed up in the shadow of the prison wall. At the appointed hour, he emerged from it to present himself in Mr. Lorry's room again, where he found the old gentleman walking to and fro in restless anxiety. He said he had been with Lucie until just now, and had only left her for a few minutes, to come and keep his appointment. Her father had not been seen, since he quitted the banking-house towards four o'clock. She had some faint hopes that his mediation might save Charles, but they were very slight. He had been more than five hours gone: where could he be?

Mr. Lorry waited until ten; but, Doctor Manette not returning, and he being unwilling to leave Lucie any longer, it was arranged that he should go back to her, and come to the banking-house again at midnight. In the meanwhile, Carton would wait alone by the fire for the Doctor.

He waited and waited, and the clock struck twelve; but Doctor Manette did not come back. Mr. Lorry returned, and found no tidings of him, and brought none. Where could he be?

They were discussing this question, and were almost building up some weak structure of hope on his prolonged absence, when they heard him on the stairs. The instant he entered the room, it was plain that all was lost.

Whether he had really been to any one, or whether he had been all that time traversing the streets, was never known. As he stood staring at them, they asked him no question, for his face told them everything.

"I cannot find it," said he, "and I must have it. Where is it?"

His head and throat were bare, and, as he spoke with a helpless look straying all around, he took his coat off, and let it drop on the floor.

"Where is my bench? I have been looking everywhere for my bench, and I can't find it. What have they done with my work? Time presses: I must finish those shoes."

They looked at one another, and their hearts died within them.

"Come, come!" said he, in a whimpering miserable way; "let me get to work. Give me my work."

Receiving no answer, he tore his hair, and beat his feet upon the ground, like a distracted child.

"Don't torture a poor forlorn wretch," he implored them, with a dreadful cry; "but give me my work! What is to become of us, if those shoes are not done to-night?"

Lost, utterly lost!

It was so clearly beyond hope to reason with him, or try to restore him, that – as if by agreement – they each put a hand upon his shoulder, and soothed him to sit down before the fire, with a promise that he should have his work presently. He sank into the chair, and brooded over the embers, and shed tears. As if all that had happened since the garret time were a momentary fancy, or a dream, Mr. Lorry saw him shrink into the exact figure that Defarge had had in keeping.

Affected, and impressed with terror as they both were, by this spectacle of ruin, it was not a time to yield to such emotions. His lonely daughter, bereft of her final hope and reliance, appealed to them both too strongly. Again, as if by agreement, they looked at one another with one meaning in their faces. Carton was the first to speak:

"The last chance is gone: it was not much. Yes; he had better be taken to her. But, before you go, will you, for a moment, steadily attend to me? Don't ask me why I make the stipulations I am going to make, and exact the promise I am going to exact; I have a reason – a good one."

"I do not doubt it," answered Mr. Lorry. "Say on."

The figure in the chair between them, was all the time monotonously rocking itself to and fro, and moaning. They spoke in such a tone as they would have used if they had been watching by a sick-bed in the night.

Carton stooped to pick up the coat, which lay almost entangling his feet. As he did so, a small case in which the Doctor was accustomed to carry the lists of his day's duties, fell lightly on the floor. Carton took it up, and there was a folded paper in it. "We should look at this!" he said. Mr. Lorry nodded his consent. He opened it, and exclaimed, "Thank **God!**"

"What is it?" asked Mr. Lorry, eagerly.

"A moment! Let me speak of it in its place. First," he put his hand in his coat, and took another paper from it, "that is the certificate which enables me to pass out of this city. Look at it. You see – Sydney Carton, an Englishman?"

Mr. Lorry held it open in his hand, gazing in his earnest face.

"Keep it for me until to-morrow. I shall see him to-morrow, you remember, and I had better not take it into the prison."

"Why not?"

"I don't know; I prefer not to do so. Now, take this paper that Doctor Manette has carried about him. It is a similar certificate, enabling him and his daughter and her child, at any time, to pass the barrier and the frontier! You see?"

"Yes!"

"Perhaps he obtained it as his last and utmost precaution against evil, yesterday. When is it dated? But no matter; don't stay to look; put it up carefully with mine and your own. Now, observe! I never doubted until within this hour or two, that he had, or could have such a paper. It is good, until recalled. But it may be soon recalled, and, I have reason to think, will be."

"They are not in danger?"

"They are in great danger. They are in danger of denunciation by Madame Defarge. I know it from her own lips. I have overheard words of that woman's, to-night, which have presented their danger to me in strong colours. I have lost no time, and since then, I have seen the spy. He confirms me. He knows that a wood-sawyer, living by the prison wall, is under the control of the Defarges, and has been rehearsed by Madame Defarge as to his having seen Her" – he never mentioned Lucie's name – "making signs and signals to prisoners. It is easy to foresee that the pretence will be the common one, a prison plot, and that it will involve her life – and perhaps her child's – and perhaps her father's – for both have been seen with her at that place. Don't look so horrified. You will save them all."

"Heaven grant I may, Carton! But how?"

"I am going to tell you how. It will depend on you, and it could depend on no better man. This new denunciation will certainly not take place until after to-morrow; probably not until two or three days afterwards; more probably a week afterwards. You know it is a capital crime, to mourn for, or sympathise with, a victim of the Guillotine. She and her father would unquestionably be guilty of this crime, and this woman (the inveteracy of whose pursuit cannot be described) would wait to add that strength to her case, and make herself doubly sure. You follow me?"

"So attentively, and with so much confidence in what you say, that for the moment I lose sight," touching the back of the Doctor's chair, "even of this distress."

"You have money, and can buy the means of travelling to the seacoast as quickly as the journey can be made. Your preparations have been completed for some days, to return to England. Early to-morrow have your horses ready, so that they may be in starting trim at two o'clock in the afternoon."

"It shall be done!"

His manner was so fervent and inspiring, that Mr. Lorry caught the flame, and was as quick as youth.

"You are a noble heart. Did I say we could depend upon no better man? Tell her, to-night, what you know of her danger as involving her child and her father. Dwell upon that, for she would lay her own fair head beside her husband's cheerfully." He faltered for an instant; then went on as before. "For the sake of her child and her father, press upon her the necessity of leaving Paris, with them and you, at that hour. Tell her that it was her husband's last arrangement. Tell her that more depends upon it than she dare believe, or hope. You think that her father, even in this sad state, will submit himself to her; do you not?"

"I am sure of it."

"I thought so. Quietly and steadily have all

these arrangements made in the courtyard here, even to the taking of your own seat in the carriage. The moment I come to you, take me in, and drive away."

"I understand that I wait for you under all circumstances?"

"You have my certificate in your hand with the rest, you know, and will reserve my place. Wait for nothing but to have my place occupied, and then for England!"

"Why, then," said Mr. Lorry, grasping his eager but so firm and steady hand, "it does not all depend on one old man, but I shall have a young and ardent man at my side."

"By the help of Heaven you shall! Promise me solemnly that nothing will influence you to alter the course on which we now stand pledged to one another."

"Nothing, Carton."

"Remember these words to-morrow: change the course, or delay in it – for any reason – and no life can possibly be saved, and many lives must inevitably be sacrificed."

"I will remember them. I hope to do my part faithfully."

"And I hope to do mine. Now, good bye!"

Though he said it with a grave smile of earnestness, and though he even put the old man's hand to his lips, he did not part from him then. He helped him so far to arouse the rocking figure before the dying embers, as to get a cloak and hat put upon it, and to tempt it forth to find where the bench and work were hidden that it still moaningly besought to have. He walked on the other side of it and protected it to the courtyard of the house where the afflicted heart – so happy in the memorable time when he had revealed his own desolate heart to it – outwatched the awful night. He entered the courtyard and remained there for a few moments alone, looking up at the light in the window of her room. Before he went away, he breathed a blessing towards it, and a Farewell.

CHAPTER THIRTEEN

Fifty-two

IN THE BLACK prison of the Conciergerie, the doomed of the day awaited their fate. They were in number as the weeks of the year. Fifty-two were to roll that afternoon on the life-tide of the city to the boundless everlasting sea. Before their cells were quit of them, new occupants were appointed; before their blood ran into the blood spilled yesterday, the blood that was to mingle with theirs to-morrow was already set apart.

Two score and twelve were told off. From the farmer-general of seventy, whose riches could not buy his life, to the seamstress of twenty, whose poverty and obscurity could not save her. Physical diseases, engendered in the vices and neglects of men, will seize on victims of all degrees; and the frightful moral disorder, born of unspeakable suffering, intolerable oppression, and heartless indifference, smote equally without distinction.

Charles Darnay, alone in a cell, had sustained himself with no flattering delusion since he came to it from the Tribunal. In every line of the narrative he had heard, he had heard his condemnation. He had fully comprehended that no personal influence could possibly save him, that he was virtually sentenced by the millions, and that units could avail him nothing.

Nevertheless, it was not easy, with the face of his beloved wife fresh before him, to compose his mind to what it must bear.

His hold on life was strong, and it was very, very hard, to loosen; by gradual efforts and degrees unclosed a little here, it clenched the tighter there; and when he brought his strength to bear on that hand and it yielded, this was closed again. There was a hurry, too, in all his thoughts, a turbulent and heated working of his heart, that contended against resignation. If, for a moment, he did feel resigned, then his wife and child who had to live after him, seemed to protest and to make it a selfish thing.

But, all this was at first. Before long, the consideration that there was no disgrace in the fate he must meet, and that numbers went the same road wrongfully, and trod it firmly every day, sprang up to stimulate him. Next followed the thought that much of the future peace of mind enjoyable by the dear ones, depended on his quiet fortitude. So, by degrees he calmed into the better state, when he could raise his thoughts much higher, and draw comfort down.

Before it had set in dark on the night of his condemnation, he had travelled thus far on his last way. Being allowed to purchase the means of writing, and a light, he sat down to write until such time as the prison lamps should be extinguished.

He wrote a long letter to Lucie, showing her that he had known nothing of her father's imprisonment, until he had heard of it from herself, and that he had been as ignorant as she of his father's and uncle's responsibility for that misery, until the paper had been read. He had already explained to her that his concealment from herself of the name he had relinquished, was the one condition – fully intelligible now – that her father had attached to their betrothal, and was the one promise he had still exacted on the morning of their marriage. He entreated her, for her father's sake, never to seek to know whether her father had become oblivious of the existence of the paper, or had had it recalled to him (for the moment, or for good), by the story of the

Tower, on that old Sunday under the dear old plane-tree in the garden. If he had preserved any definite remembrance of it, there could be no doubt that he had supposed it destroyed with the Bastille, when he had found no mention of it among the relics of prisoners which the populace had discovered there, and which had been described to all the world. He besought her – though he added that he knew it was needless – to console her father, by impressing him through every tender means she could think of, with the truth that he had done nothing for which he could justly reproach himself, but had uniformly forgotten himself for their joint sakes. Next to her preservation of his own last grateful love and blessing, and her overcoming of her sorrow, to devote herself to their dear child, he adjured her, as they would meet in Heaven, to comfort her father.

To her father himself, he wrote in the same strain; but, he told her father that he expressly confided his wife and child to his care. And he told him this, very strongly, with the hope of rousing him from any despondency or dangerous retrospect towards which he foresaw he might be tending.

To Mr. Lorry, he commended them all, and explained his worldly affairs. That done, with many added sentences of grateful friendship and warm attachment, all was done. He never thought of Carton. His mind was so full of the others, that he never once thought of him.

He had time to finish these letters before the lights were put out. When he lay down on his straw bed, he thought he had done with this world.

But, it beckoned him back in his sleep, and showed itself in shining forms. Free and happy, back in the old house in Soho (though it had nothing in it like the real house), unaccountably released and light of heart, he was with Lucie again, and she told him it was all a dream, and he had never gone away. A pause of forgetfulness, and then he had even suffered, and had come back to her, dead and at peace, and yet there was no difference in him. Another pause of oblivion, and he awoke in the sombre morning, unconscious where he was or what had happened, until it flashed upon his mind, “this is the day of my death!”

Thus, had he come through the hours, to the day when the fifty-two heads were to fall. And now, while he was composed, and hoped that he could meet the end with quiet heroism, a new action began in his waking thoughts, which was very difficult to master.

He had never seen the instrument that was to terminate his life. How high it was from the ground, how many steps it had, where he would be stood, how he would be touched, whether the touching hands would be dyed red, which way his face would be turned, whether he would be the first, or might be the last: these and many similar questions, in nowise directed by his will, obtruded themselves over and over again, countless times. Neither were they connected with fear: he was conscious of no fear. Rather, they originated in a strange besetting desire to know what to do when the time came; a desire gigantically disproportionate to the few swift moments to which it referred; a wondering that was more like the wondering of some other spirit within his, than his own.

The hours went on as he walked to and fro, and the clocks struck the numbers he would never hear again. Nine gone for ever, ten gone for ever, eleven gone for ever, twelve coming on to pass away. After a hard contest with that eccentric action of thought which had last perplexed him, he had got the better of it. He walked up and down, softly repeating their names to himself. The worst of the strife was over. He could walk up and down, free from distracting fancies, praying for himself and for them.

Twelve gone for ever.

He had been apprised that the final hour was Three, and he knew he would be summoned some time earlier, inasmuch as the tumbrils jolted heavily and slowly through the streets. Therefore, he resolved to keep Two before his mind, as the hour, and so to strengthen himself in the interval that he might be able, after that time, to strengthen others.

Walking regularly to and fro with his arms folded on his breast, a very different man from the prisoner, who had walked to and fro at La Force, he heard One struck away from him, without surprise. The hour had measured like most other hours. Devoutly thankful to Heaven for his recovered self-possession, he thought, “There is but another now,” and turned to walk again.

Footsteps in the stone passage outside the door. He stopped.

The key was put in the lock, and turned. Before the door was opened, or as it opened, a man said in a low voice, in English: “He has never seen me here; I have kept out of his way. Go you in alone; I wait near. Lose no time!”

The door was quickly opened and closed, and there stood before him face to face, quiet, intent upon him, with the light of a smile on his features, and a cautionary finger on his lip, Sydney Carton.

There was something so bright and remarkable in his look, that, for the first moment, the prisoner misdoubted him to be an apparition of his own imagining. But, he spoke, and it was his voice; he took the prisoner’s hand, and it was his real grasp.

“Of all the people upon earth, you least expected to see me?” he said.

“I could not believe it to be you. I can scarcely believe it now. You are not” – the apprehension came suddenly into his mind – ”a prisoner?”

“No. I am accidentally possessed of a power over one of the keepers here, and in virtue of it I stand before you. I come from her – your wife, dear Darnay.”

The prisoner wrung his hand.

"I bring you a request from her."

"What is it?"

"A most earnest, pressing, and emphatic entreaty, addressed to you in the most pathetic tones of the voice so dear to you, that you well remember."

The prisoner turned his face partly aside.

"You have no time to ask me why I bring it, or what it means; I have no time to tell you. You must comply with it – take off those boots you wear, and draw on these of mine."

There was a chair against the wall of the cell, behind the prisoner. Carton, pressing forward, had already, with the speed of lightning, got him down into it, and stood over him, barefoot.

"Draw on these boots of mine. Put your hands to them; put your will to them. Quick!"

"Carton, there is no escaping from this place; it never can be done. You will only die with me. It is madness."

"It would be madness if I asked you to escape; but do I? When I ask you to pass out at that door, tell me it is madness and remain here. Change that cravat for this of mine, that coat for this of mine. While you do it, let me take this ribbon from your hair, and shake out your hair like this of mine!"

With wonderful quickness, and with a strength both of will and action, that appeared quite supernatural, he forced all these changes upon him. The prisoner was like a young child in his hands.

"Carton! Dear Carton! It is madness. It cannot be accomplished, it never can be done, it has been attempted, and has always failed. I implore you not to add your death to the bitterness of mine."

"Do I ask you, my dear Darnay, to pass the door? When I ask that, refuse. There are pen and ink and paper on this table. Is your hand steady enough to write?"

"It was when you came in."

"Steady it again, and write what I shall dictate. Quick, friend, quick!"

Pressing his hand to his bewildered head,

Darnay sat down at the table. Carton, with his right hand in his breast, stood close beside him.

"Write exactly as I speak."

"To whom do I address it?"

"To no one." Carton still had his hand in his breast.

"Do I date it?"

"No."

The prisoner looked up, at each question. Carton, standing over him with his hand in his breast, looked down.

"'If you remember,'" said Carton, dictating, "'the words that passed between us, long ago, you will readily comprehend this when you see it. You do remember them, I know. It is not in your nature to forget them.'"

He was drawing his hand from his breast; the prisoner chancing to look up in his hurried wonder as he wrote, the hand stopped, closing upon something.

"Have you written 'forget them'?" Carton asked.

"I have. Is that a weapon in your hand?"

"No; I am not armed."

"What is it in your hand?"

"You shall know directly. Write on; there are but a few words more." He dictated again. "'I am thankful that the time has come, when I can prove them. That I do so is no subject for regret or grief.'" As he said these words with his eyes fixed on the writer, his hand slowly and softly moved down close to the writer's face.

The pen dropped from Darnay's fingers on the table, and he looked about him vacantly.

"What vapour is that?" he asked.

"Vapour?"

"Something that crossed me?"

"I am conscious of nothing; there can be nothing here. Take up the pen and finish. Hurry, hurry!"

As if his memory were impaired, or his faculties disordered, the prisoner made an effort to rally his attention. As he looked at Carton with clouded eyes and with an altered manner of breathing, Carton – his hand again in his breast – looked steadily at him.

"Hurry, hurry!"

The prisoner bent over the paper, once more.

"'If it had been otherwise;'" Carton's hand was again watchfully and softly stealing down; "'I never should have used the longer opportunity. If it had been otherwise;'" the hand was at the prisoner's face; "'I should but have had so much the more to answer for. If it had been otherwise – '" Carton looked at the pen and saw it was trailing off into unintelligible signs.

Carton's hand moved back to his breast no more. The prisoner sprang up with a reproachful look, but Carton's hand was close and firm at his nostrils, and Carton's left arm caught him round the waist. For a few seconds he faintly struggled with the man who had come to lay down his life for him; but, within a minute or so, he was stretched insensible on the ground.

Quickly, but with hands as true to the purpose as his heart was, Carton dressed himself in the clothes the prisoner had laid aside, combed back his hair, and tied it with the ribbon the prisoner had worn. Then, he softly called, “Enter there! Come in!” and the Spy presented himself.

“You see?” said Carton, looking up, as he kneeled on one knee beside the insensible figure, putting the paper in the breast: “is your hazard very great?”

“Mr. Carton,” the Spy answered, with a timid snap of his fingers, “my hazard is not **that**, in the thick of business here, if you are true to the whole of your bargain.”

“Don’t fear me. I will be true to the death.”

“You must be, Mr. Carton, if the tale of fifty-two is to be right. Being made right by you in that dress, I shall have no fear.”

“Have no fear! I shall soon be out of the way of harming you, and the rest will soon be far from here, please God! Now, get assistance and take me to the coach."

"You?" said the Spy nervously.

"Him, man, with whom I have exchanged. You go out at the gate by which you brought me in?"

"Of course."

"I was weak and faint when you brought me in, and I am fainter now you take me out. The parting interview has overpowered me. Such a thing has happened here, often, and too often. Your life is in your own hands. Quick! Call assistance!"

"You swear not to betray me?" said the trembling Spy, as he paused for a last moment.

"Man, man!" returned Carton, stamping his foot; "have I sworn by no solemn vow already, to go through with this, that you waste the precious moments now? Take him yourself to the courtyard you know of, place him yourself in the carriage, show him yourself to Mr. Lorry, tell him yourself to give him no restorative but air, and to remember my words of last night, and his promise of last night, and drive away!"

The Spy withdrew, and Carton seated himself at the table, resting his forehead on his hands. The Spy returned immediately, with two men.

"How, then?" said one of them, contemplating the fallen figure. "So afflicted to find that his friend has drawn a prize in the lottery of Sainte Guillotine?"

"A good patriot," said the other, "could hardly have been more afflicted if the Aristocrat had drawn a blank."

They raised the unconscious figure, placed it on a litter they had brought to the door, and bent to carry it away.

"The time is short, Evremonde," said the Spy, in a warning voice.

"I know it well," answered Carton. "Be careful of my friend, I entreat you, and leave me."

"Come, then, my children," said Barsad. "Lift him, and come away!"

The door closed, and Carton was left alone. Straining his powers of listening to the utmost, he listened for any sound that might denote suspicion or alarm. There was none. Keys turned, doors clashed, footsteps passed along distant passages: no cry was raised, or hurry made, that seemed unusual. Breathing more freely in a little while, he sat down at the table, and listened again until the clock struck Two.

Sounds that he was not afraid of, for he divined their meaning, then began to be audible. Several doors were opened in succession, and finally his own. A gaoler, with a list in his hand, looked in, merely saying, "Follow me, Evremonde!" and he followed into a large dark room, at a distance. It was a dark winter day, and what with the shadows within, and what with the shadows without, he could but dimly discern the others who were brought there to have their arms bound. Some were standing; some seated. Some were lamenting, and in restless motion; but, these were few. The great majority were silent and still, looking fixedly at the ground.

As he stood by the wall in a dim corner, while some of the fifty-two were brought in after him, one man stopped in passing, to embrace him, as having a knowledge of him. It thrilled him with a great dread of discovery; but the man went on. A very few moments after that, a young woman, with a slight girlish form, a sweet spare face in which there was no vestige of colour, and large widely opened patient eyes, rose from the seat where he had observed her sitting, and came to speak to him.

"Citizen Evremonde," she said, touching him with her cold hand. "I am a poor little seamstress, who was with you in La Force."

He murmured for answer: "True. I forget what you were accused of?"

"Plots. Though the just Heaven knows that I am innocent of any. Is it likely? Who would think of plotting with a poor little weak creature like me?"

The forlorn smile with which she said it, so touched him, that tears started from his eyes.

"I am not afraid to die, Citizen Evremonde, but I have done nothing. I am not unwilling to die, if the Republic which is to do so much good to us poor, will profit by my death; but I do not know how that can be, Citizen Evremonde. Such a poor weak little creature!"

As the last thing on earth that his heart was to warm and soften to, it warmed and softened to this pitiable girl.

"I heard you were released, Citizen Evremonde. I hoped it was true?"

"It was. But, I was again taken and condemned."

"If I may ride with you, Citizen Evremonde, will you let me hold your hand? I am not afraid, but I am little and weak, and it will give me more courage."

As the patient eyes were lifted to his face, he saw a sudden doubt in them, and then astonishment. He pressed the work-worn, hunger-worn young fingers, and touched his lips.

"Are you dying for him?" she whispered.

"And his wife and child. Hush! Yes."

"O you will let me hold your brave hand, stranger?"

"Hush! Yes, my poor sister; to the last."

The same shadows that are falling on the prison, are falling, in that same hour of the early afternoon, on the Barrier with the crowd about it, when a coach going out of Paris drives up to be examined.

"Who goes here? Whom have we within? Papers!"

The papers are handed out, and read.

"Alexandre Manette. Physician. French. Which is he?"

This is he; this helpless, inarticulately murmuring, wandering old man pointed out.

"Apparently the Citizen-Doctor is not in his right mind? The Revolution-fever will have been too much for him?"

Greatly too much for him.

"Hah! Many suffer with it. Lucie. His daughter. French. Which is she?"

This is she.

"Apparently it must be. Lucie, the wife of Evremonde; is it not?"

It is.

"Hah! Evremonde has an assignation elsewhere. Lucie, her child. English. This is she?"

She and no other.

"Kiss me, child of Evremonde. Now, thou hast kissed a good Republican; something new in thy family; remember it! Sydney Carton. Advocate. English. Which is he?"

He lies here, in this corner of the carriage. He, too, is pointed out.

"Apparently the English advocate is in a swoon?"

It is hoped he will recover in the fresher air. It is represented that he is not in strong health, and has separated sadly from a friend who is under the displeasure of the Republic.

"Is that all? It is not a great deal, that! Many are under the displeasure of the Republic, and must look out at the little window. Jarvis Lorry. Banker. English. Which is he?"

"I am he. Necessarily, being the last."

It is Jarvis Lorry who has replied to all the previous questions. It is Jarvis Lorry who has alighted and stands with his hand on the coach door, replying to a group of officials. They leisurely walk round the carriage and leisurely mount the box, to look at what little luggage it carries on the roof; the country-people hanging about, press nearer to the coach doors and greedily stare in; a little child, carried by its mother, has its short arm held out for it, that it may touch the wife of an aristocrat who has gone to the Guillotine.

"Behold your papers, Jarvis Lorry, countersigned."

"One can depart, citizen?"

"One can depart. Forward, my postilions!

A good journey!"

"I salute you, citizens. –And the first danger passed!"

These are again the words of Jarvis Lorry, as he clasps his hands, and looks upward. There is terror in the carriage, there is weeping, there is the heavy breathing of the insensible traveller.

"Are we not going too slowly? Can they not be induced to go faster?" asks Lucie, clinging to the old man.

"It would seem like flight, my darling. I must not urge them too much; it would rouse suspicion."

"Look back, look back, and see if we are pursued!"

"The road is clear, my dearest. So far, we are not pursued."

Houses in twos and threes pass by us, solitary farms, ruinous buildings, dye-works, tanneries, and the like, open country, avenues of leafless trees. The hard uneven pavement is under us, the soft deep mud is on either side. Sometimes, we strike into the skirting mud, to avoid the stones that clatter us and shake us; sometimes, we stick in ruts and sloughs there. The agony of our impatience is then so great, that in our wild alarm and hurry we are for getting out and running – hiding – doing anything but stopping.

Out of the open country, in again among ruinous buildings, solitary farms, dye-works, tanneries, and the like, cottages in twos and threes, avenues of leafless trees. Have these men deceived us, and taken us back by another road? Is not this the same place twice over? Thank Heaven, no. A village. Look back, look back, and see if we are pursued! Hush! the posting-house.

Leisurely, our four horses are taken out; leisurely, the coach stands in the little street, bereft of horses, and with no likelihood upon it of ever moving again; leisurely, the new horses come into visible existence, one by one; leisurely, the new postilions follow, sucking and plaiting the lashes of their whips; leisurely, the old postilions count their money, make wrong additions, and arrive at dissatisfied results. All the time, our overfraught hearts are beating at a rate that would far outstrip the fastest gallop of the fastest horses ever foaled.

At length the new postilions are in their saddles, and the old are left behind. We are through the village, up the hill, and down the hill, and on the low watery grounds. Suddenly, the postilions exchange speech with animated gesticulation, and the horses are pulled up, almost on their haunches. We are pursued?

"Ho! Within the carriage there. Speak then!"

"What is it?" asks Mr. Lorry, looking out at window.

"How many did they say?"

"I do not understand you."

" – At the last post. How many to the Guillotine to-day?"

"Fifty-two."

"I said so! A brave number! My fellow-citizen here would have it forty-two; ten more heads are worth having. The Guillotine goes handsomely. I love it. Hi forward. Whoop!"

The night comes on dark. He moves more; he is beginning to revive, and to speak intelligibly; he thinks they are still together; he asks him, by his name, what he has in his hand. O pity us, kind Heaven, and help us! Look out, look out, and see if we are pursued.

The wind is rushing after us, and the clouds are flying after us, and the moon is plunging after us, and the whole wild night is in pursuit of us; but, so far, we are pursued by nothing else.

CHAPTER FOURTEEN

The Knitting Done

IN THAT SAME juncture of time when the Fifty-Two awaited their fate Madame Defarge held darkly ominous council with The Vengeance and Jacques Three of the Revolutionary Jury. Not in the wine-shop did Madame Defarge confer with these ministers, but in the shed of the wood-sawyer, erst a mender of roads. The sawyer himself did not participate in the conference, but abided at a little distance, like an outer satellite who was not to speak until required, or to offer an opinion until invited.

"But our Defarge," said Jacques Three, "is undoubtedly a good Republican? Eh?"

"There is no better," the voluble Vengeance protested in her shrill notes, "in France."

"Peace, little Vengeance," said Madame Defarge, laying her hand with a slight frown on her lieutenant's lips, "hear me speak. My husband, fellow-citizen, is a good Republican and a bold man; he has deserved well of the Republic, and possesses its confidence. But my husband has his weaknesses, and he is so weak as to relent towards this Doctor."

"It is a great pity," croaked Jacques Three, dubiously shaking his head, with his cruel fingers at his hungry mouth; "it is not quite like a good citizen; it is a thing to regret."

"See you," said madame, "I care nothing for this Doctor, I. He may wear his head or lose it, for any interest I have in him; it is all one to me. But, the Evremonde people are to be exterminated, and the wife and child must follow the husband and father."

"She has a fine head for it," croaked Jacques Three. "I have seen blue eyes and golden hair there, and they looked charming when Samson held them up." Ogre that he was, he spoke like an epicure.

Madame Defarge cast down her eyes, and reflected a little.

"The child also," observed Jacques Three, with a meditative enjoyment of his words, "has golden hair and blue eyes. And we seldom have a child there. It is a pretty sight!"

"In a word," said Madame Defarge, coming out of her short abstraction, "I cannot trust my husband in this matter. Not only do I feel, since last night, that I dare not confide to him the details of my projects; but also I feel that if I delay, there is danger of his giving warning, and then they might escape."

"That must never be," croaked Jacques Three; "no one must escape. We have not half enough as it is. We ought to have six score a day."

"In a word," Madame Defarge went on, "my husband has not my reason for pursuing this family to annihilation, and I have not his reason for regarding this Doctor with any sensibility. I must act for myself, therefore. Come hither, little citizen."

The wood-sawyer, who held her in the respect, and himself in the submission, of mortal fear, advanced with his hand to his red cap.

"Touching those signals, little citizen," said Madame Defarge, sternly, "that she made to the prisoners; you are ready to bear witness to them this very day?"

"Ay, ay, why not!" cried the sawyer. "Every day, in all weathers, from two to four, always signalling, sometimes with the little one, sometimes without. I know what I know. I have seen with my eyes."

He made all manner of gestures while he spoke, as if in incidental imitation of some few of the great diversity of signals that he had never seen.

“Clearly plots,” said Jacques Three. “Transparently!”

“There is no doubt of the Jury?” inquired Madame Defarge, letting her eyes turn to him with a gloomy smile.

“Rely upon the patriotic Jury, dear citizeness. I answer for my fellow-Jurymen.”

“Now, let me see,” said Madame Defarge, pondering again. “Yet once more! Can I spare this Doctor to my husband? I have no feeling either way. Can I spare him?”

“He would count as one head,” observed Jacques Three, in a low voice. “We really have not heads enough; it would be a pity, I think.”

“He was signalling with her when I saw her,” argued Madame Defarge; “I cannot speak of one without the other; and I must not be silent, and trust the case wholly to him, this little citizen here. For, I am not a bad witness.”

The Vengeance and Jacques Three vied with each other in their fervent protestations that she was the most admirable and marvellous of witnesses. The little citizen, not to be outdone, declared her to be a celestial witness.

"He must take his chance," said Madame Defarge. "No, I cannot spare him! You are engaged at three o'clock; you are going to see the batch of to-day executed. – You?"

The question was addressed to the wood-sawyer, who hurriedly replied in the affirmative: seizing the occasion to add that he was the most ardent of Republicans, and that he would be in effect the most desolate of Republicans, if anything prevented him from enjoying the pleasure of smoking his afternoon pipe in the contemplation of the droll national barber. He was so very demonstrative herein, that he might have been suspected (perhaps was, by the dark eyes that looked contemptuously at him out of Madame Defarge's head) of having his small individual fears for his own personal safety, every hour in the day.

"I," said madame, "am equally engaged at the same place. After it is over – say at eight to-night – come you to me, in Saint Antoine, and we will give information against these people at my Section."

The wood-sawyer said he would be proud and flattered to attend the citizeness. The citizeness looking at him, he became embarrassed, evaded her glance as a small dog would have done, retreated among his wood, and hid his confusion over the handle of his saw.

Madame Defarge beckoned the Juryman and The Vengeance a little nearer to the door, and there expounded her further views to them thus:

"She will now be at home, awaiting the moment of his death. She will be mourning and grieving. She will be in a state of mind to impeach the justice of the Republic. She will be full of sympathy with its enemies. I will go to her."

"What an admirable woman; what an adorable woman!" exclaimed Jacques Three, rapturously. "Ah, my cherished!" cried The Vengeance; and embraced her.

"Take you my knitting," said Madame Defarge, placing it in her lieutenant's hands, "and have it ready for me in my usual seat. Keep me my usual chair. Go you there, straight, for there will probably be a greater concourse than usual, to-day."

"I willingly obey the orders of my Chief," said The Vengeance with alacrity, and kissing her cheek. "You will not be late?"

"I shall be there before the commencement."

"And before the tumbrils arrive. Be sure you are there, my soul," said The Vengeance, calling after her, for she had already turned into the street, "before the tumbrils arrive!"

Madame Defarge slightly waved her hand, to imply that she heard, and might be relied upon to arrive in good time, and so went through the mud, and round the corner of the prison wall. The Vengeance and the Juryman, looking after her as she walked away, were highly appreciative of her fine figure, and her superb moral endowments.

There were many women at that time, upon whom the time laid a dreadfully disfiguring hand; but, there was not one among them more to be dreaded than this ruthless woman, now taking her way along the streets. Of a strong and fearless character, of shrewd sense and readiness, of great determination, of that kind of beauty which not only seems to impart to its possessor firmness and animosity, but to strike into others an instinctive recognition of those qualities; the troubled time would have heaved her up, under any circumstances. But, imbued from her childhood with a brooding sense of wrong, and an inveterate hatred of a class, opportunity had developed her into a tigress. She was absolutely without pity. If she had ever had the virtue in her, it had quite gone out of her.

It was nothing to her, that an innocent man was to die for the sins of his forefathers; she saw, not him, but them. It was nothing to her, that his wife was to be made a widow and his daughter an orphan; that was insufficient punishment, because they were her natural enemies and her prey, and as such had no right to live. To appeal to her, was made hopeless by her having no sense of pity, even for herself. If she had been laid low in the streets, in any of the many encounters in which she had been engaged, she would not have pitied herself; nor, if she had been ordered to the axe to-morrow, would she have gone to it with any softer feeling than a fierce desire to change places with the man who sent her there.

Such a heart Madame Defarge carried under her rough robe. Carelessly worn, it was a becoming robe enough, in a certain weird way, and her dark hair looked rich under her coarse red cap. Lying hidden in her bosom, was a loaded pistol. Lying hidden at her waist, was a sharpened dagger. Thus accoutred, and walking with the confident tread of such a character, and with the supple freedom of a woman who had habitually walked in her girlhood, bare-foot and bare-legged, on the brown sea-sand, Madame Defarge took her way along the streets.

Now, when the journey of the travelling coach, at that very moment waiting for the completion of its load, had been planned out last night, the difficulty of taking Miss Pross in it had much engaged Mr. Lorry's attention. It was not merely desirable to avoid overloading the coach, but it was of the highest importance that the time occupied in examining it and its passengers, should be reduced to the utmost; since their escape might depend on the saving of only a few seconds here and there. Finally, he had proposed, after anxious consideration, that Miss Pross and Jerry, who were at liberty to leave the city, should leave it at three o'clock in the lightest-wheeled conveyance known to that period. Unencumbered with luggage, they would soon overtake the coach, and, passing it and preceding it on the road, would order its horses in advance, and greatly facilitate its progress during the precious hours of the night, when delay was the most to be dreaded.

Seeing in this arrangement the hope of rendering real service in that pressing emergency, Miss Pross hailed it with joy. She and Jerry had beheld the coach start, had known who it was that Solomon brought, had passed some ten minutes in tortures of suspense, and were now concluding their arrangements to follow the coach, even as Madame Defarge, taking her way through the streets, now drew nearer and nearer to the else-deserted lodging in which they held their consultation.

"Now what do you think, Mr. Cruncher," said Miss Pross, whose agitation was so great that she could hardly speak, or stand, or move, or live: “what do you think of our not starting from this courtyard? Another carriage having already gone from here to-day, it might awaken suspicion.”

“My opinion, miss,” returned Mr. Cruncher, “is as you’re right. Likewise wot I’ll stand by you, right or wrong.”

“I am so distracted with fear and hope for our precious creatures,” said Miss Pross, wildly crying, “that I am incapable of forming any plan. Are **you** capable of forming any plan, my dear good Mr. Cruncher?”

“Respectin’ a future spear o’ life, miss,” returned Mr. Cruncher, “I hope so. Respectin’ any present use o’ this here blessed old head o’ mine, I think not. Would you do me the favour, miss, to take notice o’ two promises and wows wot it is my wishes fur to record in this here crisis?”

“Oh, for gracious sake!” cried Miss Pross, still wildly crying, “record them at once, and get them out of the way, like an excellent man.”

"First," said Mr. Cruncher, who was all in a tremble, and who spoke with an ashy and solemn visage, "them poor things well out o' this, never no more will I do it, never no more!"

"I am quite sure, Mr. Cruncher," returned Miss Pross, "that you never will do it again, whatever it is, and I beg you not to think it necessary to mention more particularly what it is."

"No, miss," returned Jerry, "it shall not be named to you. Second: them poor things well out o' this, and never no more will I interfere with Mrs. Cruncher's flopping, never no more!"

"Whatever housekeeping arrangement that may be," said Miss Pross, striving to dry her eyes and compose herself, "I have no doubt it is best that Mrs. Cruncher should have it entirely under her own superintendence. – O my poor darlings!"

"I go so far as to say, miss, moreover," proceeded Mr. Cruncher, with a most alarming tendency to hold forth as from a pulpit – "and let my words be took down and took to Mrs. Cruncher through yourself – that wot my opinions respectin' flopping has undergone a change, and that wot I only hope with all my heart as Mrs. Cruncher may be a flopping at the present time."

"There, there, there! I hope she is, my dear man," cried the distracted Miss Pross, "and I hope she finds it answering her expectations."

"Forbid it," proceeded Mr. Cruncher, with additional solemnity, additional slowness, and additional tendency to hold forth and hold out, "as anything wot I have ever said or done should be wisited on my earnest wishes for them poor creeturs now! Forbid it as we shouldn't all flop (if it was anyways conwenient) to get 'em out o' this here dismal risk! Forbid it, miss! Wot I say, for-**bid** it!" This was Mr. Cruncher's conclusion after a protracted but vain endeavour to find a better one.

And still Madame Defarge, pursuing her way along the streets, came nearer and nearer.

"If we ever get back to our native land," said Miss Pross, "you may rely upon my telling Mrs. Cruncher as much as I may be able to remember and understand of what you have so impressively said; and at all events you may be sure that I shall bear witness to your being thoroughly in earnest at this dreadful time. Now, pray let us think! My esteemed Mr. Cruncher, let us think!"

Still, Madame Defarge, pursuing her way along the streets, came nearer and nearer.

"If you were to go before," said Miss Pross, "and stop the vehicle and horses from coming here, and were to wait somewhere for me; wouldn't that be best?"

Mr. Cruncher thought it might be best.

"Where could you wait for me?" asked Miss Pross.

Mr. Cruncher was so bewildered that he could think of no locality but Temple Bar.

Alas! Temple Bar was hundreds of miles away, and Madame Defarge was drawing very near indeed.

"By the cathedral door," said Miss Pross. "Would it be much out of the way, to take me in, near the great cathedral door between the two towers?"

"No, miss," answered Mr. Cruncher.

"Then, like the best of men," said Miss Pross, "go to the posting-house straight, and make that change."

"I am doubtful," said Mr. Cruncher, hesitating and shaking his head, "about leaving of you, you see. We don't know what may happen."

"Heaven knows we don't," returned Miss Pross, "but have no fear for me. Take me in at the cathedral, at Three o'Clock, or as near it as you can, and I am sure it will be better than our going from here. I feel certain of it. There! Bless you, Mr. Cruncher! Think-not of me, but of the lives that may depend on both of us!"

This exordium, and Miss Pross's two hands in quite agonised entreaty clasping his, decided Mr. Cruncher. With an encouraging nod or two, he immediately went out to alter the arrangements, and left her by herself to follow as she had proposed.

The having originated a precaution which was already in course of execution, was a great relief to Miss Pross. The necessity of composing her appearance so that it should attract no special notice in the streets, was another relief. She looked at her watch, and it was twenty minutes past two. She had no time to lose, but must get ready at once.

Afraid, in her extreme perturbation, of the loneliness of the deserted rooms, and of half-imagined faces peeping from behind every open door in them, Miss Pross got a basin of cold water and began laving her eyes, which were swollen and red. Haunted by her feverish apprehensions, she could not bear to have her sight obscured for a minute at a time by the dripping water, but constantly paused and looked round to see that there was no one watching her. In one of those pauses she recoiled and cried out, for she saw a figure standing in the room.

The basin fell to the ground broken, and the water flowed to the feet of Madame Defarge. By strange stern ways, and through much staining blood, those feet had come to meet that water.

Madame Defarge looked coldly at her, and said, “The wife of Evremonde; where is she?”

It flashed upon Miss Pross’s mind that the doors were all standing open, and would suggest the flight. Her first act was to shut them. There were four in the room, and she shut them all. She then placed herself before the door of the chamber which Lucie had occupied.

Madame Defarge’s dark eyes followed her through this rapid movement, and rested on her when it was finished. Miss Pross had nothing beautiful about her; years had not tamed the wildness, or softened the grimness, of her appearance; but, she too was a determined woman in her different way, and she measured Madame Defarge with her eyes, every inch.

"You might, from your appearance, be the wife of Lucifer," said Miss Pross, in her breathing. "Nevertheless, you shall not get the better of me. I am an Englishwoman."

Madame Defarge looked at her scornfully, but still with something of Miss Pross's own perception that they two were at bay. She saw a tight, hard, wiry woman before her, as Mr. Lorry had seen in the same figure a woman with a strong hand, in the years gone by. She knew full well that Miss Pross was the family's devoted friend; Miss Pross knew full well that Madame Defarge was the family's malevolent enemy.

"On my way yonder," said Madame Defarge, with a slight movement of her hand towards the fatal spot, "where they reserve my chair and my knitting for me, I am come to make my compliments to her in passing. I wish to see her."

"I know that your intentions are evil," said Miss Pross, "and you may depend upon it, I'll hold my own against them."

Each spoke in her own language; neither understood the other's words; both were very watchful, and intent to deduce from look and manner, what the unintelligible words meant.

"It will do her no good to keep herself concealed from me at this moment," said Madame Defarge. "Good patriots will know what that means. Let me see her. Go tell her that I wish to see her. Do you hear?"

"If those eyes of yours were bed-winches," returned Miss Pross, "and I was an English four-poster, they shouldn't loose a splinter of me. No, you wicked foreign woman; I am your match."

Madame Defarge was not likely to follow these idiomatic remarks in detail; but, she so far understood them as to perceive that she was set at naught.

"Woman imbecile and pig-like!" said Madame Defarge, frowning. "I take no answer from you. I demand to see her. Either tell her that I demand to see her, or stand out of the way of the door and let me go to her!" This, with an angry explanatory wave of her right arm.

"I little thought," said Miss Pross, "that I should ever want to understand your nonsensical language; but I would give all I have, except the clothes I wear, to know whether you suspect the truth, or any part of it."

Neither of them for a single moment released the other's eyes. Madame Defarge had not moved from the spot where she stood when Miss Pross first became aware of her; but, she now advanced one step.

"I am a Briton," said Miss Pross, "I am desperate. I don't care an English Twopence for myself. I know that the longer I keep you here, the greater hope there is for my Ladybird. I'll not leave a handful of that dark hair upon your head, if you lay a finger on me!"

Thus Miss Pross, with a shake of her head and a flash of her eyes between every rapid sentence, and every rapid sentence a whole breath. Thus Miss Pross, who had never struck a blow in her life.

But, her courage was of that emotional nature that it brought the irrepressible tears into her eyes. This was a courage that Madame Defarge so little comprehended as to mistake for weakness. "Ha, ha!" she laughed, "you poor wretch! What are you worth! I address myself to that Doctor." Then she raised her voice and called out, "Citizen Doctor! Wife of Evremonde! Child of Evremonde! Any person but this miserable fool, answer the Citizeness Defarge!"

Perhaps the following silence, perhaps some latent disclosure in the expression of Miss Pross's face, perhaps a sudden misgiving apart from either suggestion, whispered to Madame Defarge that they were gone. Three of the doors she opened swiftly, and looked in.

"Those rooms are all in disorder, there has been hurried packing, there are odds and ends upon the ground. There is no one in that room behind you! Let me look."

"Never!" said Miss Pross, who understood the request as perfectly as Madame Defarge understood the answer.

"If they are not in that room, they are gone, and can be pursued and brought back," said Madame Defarge to herself.

"As long as you don't know whether they are in that room or not, you are uncertain what to do," said Miss Pross to herself; "and you shall not know that, if I can prevent your knowing it; and know that, or not know that, you shall not leave here while I can hold you."

"I have been in the streets from the first, nothing has stopped me, I will tear you to pieces, but I will have you from that door," said Madame Defarge.

"We are alone at the top of a high house in a solitary courtyard, we are not likely to be heard, and I pray for bodily strength to keep you here, while every minute you are here is worth a hundred thousand guineas to my darling," said Miss Pross.

Madame Defarge made at the door. Miss Pross, on the instinct of the moment, seized her round the waist in both her arms, and held her tight. It was in vain for Madame Defarge to struggle and to strike; Miss Pross, with the vigorous tenacity of love, always so much stronger than hate, clasped her tight, and even lifted her from the floor in the struggle that they had. The two hands of Madame Defarge buffeted and tore her face; but, Miss Pross, with her head down, held her round the waist, and clung to her with more than the hold of a drowning woman.

Soon, Madame Defarge's hands ceased to strike, and felt at her encircled waist.

"It is under my arm," said Miss Pross, in smothered tones, "you shall not draw it. I am stronger than you, I bless Heaven for it. I hold you till one or other of us faints or dies!"

Madame Defarge's hands were at her bosom. Miss Pross looked up, saw what it was, struck at it, struck out a flash and a crash, and stood alone – blinded with smoke.

All this was in a second. As the smoke cleared, leaving an awful stillness, it passed out on the air, like the soul of the furious woman whose body lay lifeless on the ground.

In the first fright and horror of her situation, Miss Pross passed the body as far from it as she could, and ran down the stairs to call for fruitless help. Happily, she bethought herself of the consequences of what she did, in time to check herself and go back. It was dreadful to go in at the door again; but, she did go in, and even went near it, to get the bonnet and other things that she must wear. These she put on, out on the staircase, first shutting and locking the door and taking away the key. She then sat down on the stairs a few moments to breathe and to cry, and then got up and hurried away.

By good fortune she had a veil on her bonnet, or she could hardly have gone along the streets without being stopped. By good fortune, too, she was naturally so peculiar in appearance as not to show disfigurement like any other woman. She needed both advantages, for the marks of gripping fingers were deep in her face, and her hair was torn, and her dress (hastily composed with unsteady hands) was clutched and dragged a hundred ways.

In crossing the bridge, she dropped the door key in the river. Arriving at the cathedral some few minutes before her escort, and waiting there, she thought, what if the key were already taken in a net, what if it were identified, what if the door were opened and the remains discovered, what if she were stopped at the gate, sent to prison, and charged with murder! In the midst of these fluttering thoughts, the escort appeared, took her in, and took her away.

"Is there any noise in the streets?" she asked him.

"The usual noises," Mr. Cruncher replied; and looked surprised by the question and by her aspect.

"I don't hear you," said Miss Pross. "What do you say?"

It was in vain for Mr. Cruncher to repeat what he said; Miss Pross could not hear him. "So I'll nod my head," thought Mr. Cruncher, amazed, "at all events she'll see that." And she did.

"Is there any noise in the streets now?" asked Miss Pross again, presently.

Again Mr. Cruncher nodded his head.

"I don't hear it."

"Gone deaf in an hour?" said Mr. Cruncher, ruminating, with his mind much disturbed;

"wot's come to her?"

"I feel," said Miss Pross, "as if there had been a flash and a crash, and that crash was the last thing I should ever hear in this life."

"Blest if she ain't in a queer condition!" said Mr. Cruncher, more and more disturbed. "Wot can she have been a takin', to keep her courage up? Hark! There's the roll of them dreadful carts! You can hear that, miss?"

"I can hear," said Miss Pross, seeing that he spoke to her, "nothing. O, my good man, there was first a great crash, and then a great stillness, and that stillness seems to be fixed and unchangeable, never to be broken any more as long as my life lasts."

"If she don't hear the roll of those dreadful carts, now very nigh their journey's end," said Mr. Cruncher, glancing over his shoulder, "it's my opinion that indeed she never will hear anything else in this world."

And indeed she never did.

CHAPTER FIFTEEN

The Footsteps Die Out For Ever

ALONG THE Paris streets, the death-carts rumble, hollow and harsh. Six tumbrils carry the day's wine to La Guillotine. All the devouring and insatiate Monsters imagined since imagination could record itself, are fused in the one realisation, Guillotine. And yet there is not in France, with its rich variety of soil and climate, a blade, a leaf, a root, a sprig, a peppercorn, which will grow to maturity under conditions more certain than those that have produced this horror. Crush humanity out of shape once more, under similar hammers, and it will twist itself into the same tortured forms. Sow the same seed of rapacious license and oppression over again, and it will surely yield the same fruit according to its kind.

Six tumbrils roll along the streets. Change these back again to what they were, thou powerful enchanter, Time, and they shall be seen to be the carriages of absolute monarchs, the equipages of feudal nobles, the toilettes of flaring Jezebels, the churches that are not my father's house but dens of thieves, the huts of millions of starving peasants! No; the great magician who majestically works out the appointed order of the Creator, never reverses his transformations. "If thou be changed into this shape by the will of God," say the seers to the enchanted, in the wise Arabian stories, "then remain so! But, if thou wear this form through mere passing conjuration, then resume thy former aspect!" Changeless and hopeless, the tumbrils roll along.

As the sombre wheels of the six carts go round, they seem to plough up a long crooked furrow among the populace in the streets. Ridges of faces are thrown to this side and to that, and the ploughs go steadily onward. So used are the regular inhabitants of the houses to the spectacle, that in many windows there are no people, and in some the occupation of the hands is not so much as suspended, while the eyes survey the faces in the tumbrils. Here and there, the inmate has visitors to see the sight; then he points his finger, with something of the complacency of a curator or authorised exponent, to this cart and to this, and seems to tell who sat here yesterday, and who there the day before.

Of the riders in the tumbrils, some observe these things, and all things on their last roadside, with an impassive stare; others, with a lingering interest in the ways of life and men. Some, seated with drooping heads, are sunk in silent despair; again, there are some so heedful of their looks that they cast upon the multitude such glances as they have seen in theatres, and in pictures. Several close their eyes, and think, or try to get their straying thoughts together. Only one, and he a miserable creature, of a crazed aspect, is so shattered and made drunk by horror, that he sings, and tries to dance. Not one of the whole number appeals by look or gesture, to the pity of the people.

There is a guard of sundry horsemen riding abreast of the tumbrils, and faces are often turned up to some of them, and they are asked some question. It would seem to be always the same question, for, it is always followed by a press of people towards the third cart. The horsemen abreast of that cart, frequently point out one man in it with their swords. The leading curiosity is, to know which is he; he stands at the back of the tumbril with his head bent down, to converse with a mere girl who sits on the side of the cart, and holds his hand. He has no curiosity or care for the scene about him, and always speaks to the girl. Here and there in the long street of St. Honore, cries are raised against him. If they move him at all, it is only to a quiet smile, as he shakes his hair a little more loosely about his face. He cannot easily touch his face, his arms being bound.

On the steps of a church, awaiting the coming-up of the tumbrils, stands the Spy and prison-sheep. He looks into the first of them: not there. He looks into the second: not there. He already asks himself, “Has he sacrificed me?” when his face clears, as he looks into the third.

“Which is Evremonde?” says a man behind him.

“That. At the back there.”

“With his hand in the girl’s?”

“Yes.”

The man cries, "Down, Evremonde! To the Guillotine all aristocrats! Down, Evremonde!"

"Hush, hush!" the Spy entreats him, timidly.

"And why not, citizen?"

"He is going to pay the forfeit: it will be paid in five minutes more. Let him be at peace."

But the man continuing to exclaim, "Down, Evremonde!" the face of Evremonde is for a moment turned towards him. Evremonde then sees the Spy, and looks attentively at him, and goes his way.

The clocks are on the stroke of three, and the furrow ploughed among the populace is turning round, to come on into the place of execution, and end. The ridges thrown to this side and to that, now crumble in and close behind the last plough as it passes on, for all are following to the Guillotine. In front of it, seated in chairs, as in a garden of public diversion, are a number of women, busily knitting. On one of the fore-most chairs, stands The Vengeance, looking about for her friend.

"Therese!" she cries, in her shrill tones. "Who has seen her? Therese Defarge!"

"She never missed before," says a knitting-woman of the sisterhood.

"No; nor will she miss now," cries The Vengeance, petulantly. "Therese."

"Louder," the woman recommends.

Ay! Louder, Vengeance, much louder, and still she will scarcely hear thee. Louder yet, Vengeance, with a little oath or so added, and yet it will hardly bring her. Send other women up and down to seek her, lingering somewhere; and yet, although the messengers have done dread deeds, it is questionable whether of their own wills they will go far enough to find her!

"Bad Fortune!" cries The Vengeance, stamping her foot in the chair, "and here are the tumbrils! And Evremonde will be despatched in a wink, and she not here! See her knitting in my hand, and her empty chair ready for her. I cry with vexation and disappointment!"

As The Vengeance descends from her elevation to do it, the tumbrils begin to discharge their loads. The ministers of Sainte Guillotine are robed and ready. Crash! – A head is held up, and the knitting-women who scarcely lifted their eyes to look at it a moment ago when it could think and speak, count One.

The second tumbril empties and moves on; the third comes up. Crash! – And the knitting-women, never faltering or pausing in their Work, count Two.

The supposed Evremonde descends, and the seamstress is lifted out next after him. He has not relinquished her patient hand in getting out, but still holds it as he promised. He gently places her with her back to the crashing engine that constantly whirrs up and falls, and she looks into his face and thanks him.

"But for you, dear stranger, I should not be so composed, for I am naturally a poor little thing, faint of heart; nor should I have been able to raise my thoughts to Him who was put to death, that we might have hope and comfort here to-day. I think you were sent to me by Heaven."

"Or you to me," says Sydney Carton. "Keep your eyes upon me, dear child, and mind no other object."

"I mind nothing while I hold your hand. I shall mind nothing when I let it go, if they are rapid."

"They will be rapid. Fear not!"

The two stand in the fast-thinning throng of victims, but they speak as if they were alone. Eye to eye, voice to voice, hand to hand, heart to heart, these two children of the Universal Mother, else so wide apart and differing, have come together on the dark highway, to repair home together, and to rest in her bosom.

"Brave and generous friend, will you let me ask you one last question? I am very ignorant, and it troubles me – just a little."

"Tell me what it is."

"I have a cousin, an only relative and an orphan, like myself, whom I love very dearly. She is five years younger than I, and she lives in a farmer's house in the south country. Poverty parted us, and she knows nothing of my fate – for I cannot write – and if I could, how should I tell her! It is better as it is."

"Yes, yes: better as it is."

"What I have been thinking as we came along, and what I am still thinking now, as I look into your kind strong face which gives me so much support, is this: – If the Republic really does good to the poor, and they come to be less hungry, and in all ways to suffer less, she may live a long time: she may even live to be old."

"What then, my gentle sister?"

"Do you think:" the uncomplaining eyes in which there is so much endurance, fill with tears, and the lips part a little more and tremble: "that it will seem long to me, while I wait for her in the better land where I trust both you and I will be mercifully sheltered?"

"It cannot be, my child; there is no Time there, and no trouble there."

"You comfort me so much! I am so ignorant. Am I to kiss you now? Is the moment come?"

"Yes."

She kisses his lips; he kisses hers; they solemnly bless each other. The spare hand does not tremble as he releases it; nothing worse than a sweet, bright constancy is in the patient face. She goes next before him – is gone; the knitting-women count Twenty-Two.

"I am the Resurrection and the Life, saith the Lord: he that believeth in me, though he were dead, yet shall he live: and whosoever liveth and believeth in me shall never die."

The murmuring of many voices, the upturning of many faces, the pressing on of many footsteps in the outskirts of the crowd, so that it swells forward in a mass, like one great heave of water, all flashes away. Twenty-Three.

They said of him, about the city that night, that it was the peacefullest man's face ever beheld there. Many added that he looked sublime and prophetic.

One of the most remarkable sufferers by the same axe – a woman – had asked at the foot of the same scaffold, not long before, to be allowed to write down the thoughts that were inspiring her. If he had given any utterance to his, and they were prophetic, they would have been these:

"I see Barsad, and Cly, Defarge, The Vengeance, the Juryman, the Judge, long ranks of the new oppressors who have risen on the destruction of the old, perishing by this retributive instrument, before it shall cease out of its present use. I see a beautiful city and a brilliant people rising from this abyss, and, in their struggles to be truly free, in their triumphs and defeats, through long years to come, I see the evil of this time and of the previous time of which this is the natural birth, gradually making expiation for itself and wearing out.

"I see the lives for which I lay down my life, peaceful, useful, prosperous and happy, in that England which I shall see no more. I see Her with a child upon her bosom, who bears my name. I see her father, aged and bent, but otherwise restored, and faithful to all men in his healing office, and at peace. I see the good old man, so long their friend, in ten years' time enriching them with all he has, and passing tranquilly to his reward.

"I see that I hold a sanctuary in their hearts, and in the hearts of their descendants, generations hence. I see her, an old woman, weeping for me on the anniversary of this day. I see her and her husband, their course done, lying side by side in their last earthly bed, and I know that each was not more honoured and held sacred in the other's soul, than I was in the souls of both.

"I see that child who lay upon her bosom and who bore my name, a man winning his way up in that path of life which once was mine. I see him winning it so well, that my name is made illustrious there by the light of his. I see the blots I threw upon it, faded away. I see him, fore-most of just judges and honoured men, bringing a boy of my name, with a forehead that I know and golden hair, to this place – then fair to look upon, with not a trace of this day's disfigurement – and I hear him tell the child my story, with a tender and a faltering voice.

"It is a far, far better thing that I do, than I have ever done; it is a far, far better rest that I go to than I have ever known."

GT GRANDTYPECLASSICS.COM

"There is no friend as loyal as a book." E. Hemingway

A Christmas Carol BY C. DICKENS
A Tale of Two Cities BY C. DICKENS
Alice in Wonderland BY L. CARROLL
Animal Farm BY G. ORWELL
Anna Karenina BY L. TOLSTOY
Anne of Green Gables BY L. M. MONTGOMERY
Black Beauty BY A. SEWELL
Frankenstein BY M. SHELLEY
Gone with the Wind BY M. MITCHELL
Great Expectations BY C. DICKENS
Grimm's Fairy Tales BY J. AND W. GRIMM
In Our Time BY E. HEMINGWAY
Jane Eyre BY C. BRONTË
Les Misérables BY V. HUGO
Little Women BY L. M. ALCOTT
Moby Dick BY H. MELVILLE
Oliver Twist BY C.DICKENS
Peter Pan BY J. M. BARRIE
Pride & Prejudice BY J. AUSTEN
Robinson Crusoe BY D. DEFOE
The Art of War BY S. TZU
The Count of Monte Cristo BY A. DUMAS
And Many More...

www.ingramcontent.com/pod-product-compliance
Lightning Source LLC
Chambersburg PA
CBHW020914310726
48980CB00011B/878/J

* 9 7 8 1 8 3 4 1 2 2 9 3 9 *